You're invited to a

# CREEPOVER ®

## It's All Downhill from Here

written by P. J. Night

**SIMON SPOTLIGHT**

New York  London  Toronto  Sydney  New Delhi

This book is a work of fiction. Any references to historical events, real people, or real locales are used fictitiously. Other names, characters, places, and incidents are the product of the author's imagination, and any resemblance to actual events or locales or persons, living or dead, is entirely coincidental.

SIMON SPOTLIGHT
An imprint of Simon & Schuster Children's Publishing Division
1230 Avenue of the Americas, New York, New York 10020
© 2012 by Simon & Schuster, Inc.
All rights reserved, including the right of reproduction in whole or in part in any form.
SIMON SPOTLIGHT and colophon are registered trademarks of Simon & Schuster, Inc.
YOU'RE INVITED TO A CREEPOVER is a registered trademark of Simon & Schuster, Inc.
Text by Michael Teitelbaum
For information about special discounts for bulk purchases, please contact Simon & Schuster Special Sales at 1-866-506-1949 or business@simonandschuster.com.
Manufactured in the United States of America 0114 OFF
10 9 8 7 6 5 4 3
ISBN 978-1-4424-5285-5
ISBN 978-1-4424-5286-2 (eBook)
Library of Congress Catalog Card Number 2012939909

# CHAPTER 1

"So, exactly how far away from home is this place?" asked Maggie Kim as she slouched down in the backseat of her parents' car. It was Thursday evening and the start of a long weekend. Maggie should have been excited, but was anything but.

The car sped along through the suburban streets. Maggie glanced out the window longingly. The first swirling flakes of snow had just begun to fall, illuminated by the bright house lights. Maggie ran her fingers through her dark, shoulder-length hair. She squirmed in her seat, her thin frame twisting to find a more comfortable position for what she was certain was going to be an endless car ride.

"Just a little more than four hours," Maggie's mother

replied cheerfully from the front passenger seat. Maggie's mom had long brown hair with strands of gray beginning to work their way in. She always wore her hair in a ponytail and preferred T-shirts and jeans to suits and high heels, when she wasn't working.

"Might as well be four days," Maggie mumbled to her best friend, Sophie Weiss, who sat in the backseat beside her. Sophie smiled, trying to make Maggie feel better. Her freckled face beamed out from under a mop of thick, curly red hair. She was taller than Maggie, despite the fact that they were the same age. In fact, their birthdays were just a couple of weeks apart.

Maggie and Sophie were seventh-grade classmates in a big middle school in a suburb of Denver, Colorado. The two were inseparable, and so when Maggie learned last night that she had to make the trek to the mountains for a long weekend, she invited Sophie along. After all, a sleepover with her best friend was better than being stuck in a strange house with only her family all weekend. She wondered how many sleepovers she and Sophie would have left together, if her parents' crazy plan went through.

"As long as the skiing rocks, I don't care how far

away it is," said Maggie's older brother, Simon. Simon was captain of his high school ski team. He lived to ski and felt most at home schussing down steep slopes.

"That's not a surprise, Simon," Maggie replied. "You spend nearly every weekend on the slopes."

"I can't believe there aren't any ski resorts up on this mountain already, Mrs. Kim," Sophie said.

"That's why this would be the perfect investment, Sophie," Mr. Kim chimed in from behind the wheel. His partially bald head gleamed in the oncoming headlights. Mr. Kim wore glasses, which rested on his slightly wrinkled face, giving him the appearance of someone older than his years. His youthful, sunny personality, however, more than made up for his appearance.

"A perfect investment in boredom," Maggie quipped. "We'll be, like, a million miles from civilization. Not to mention all my friends." She reached around Sophie's shoulder and gave her a hug.

"What friends?" Simon teased.

"Shut up," Maggie shot back. "All you care about is that this place has mountains and snow. You don't care about people."

"Sure I do, Mags," Simon said. "People have to make the skis, and run the lifts, and—"

"You'll be able to visit your friends on the weekends, honey," Mrs. Kim interrupted, knowing that the current backseat conversation could only move in one direction—escalation into full-fledged sibling warfare.

"I've managed somebody else's hotel for years," Mr. Kim pointed out.

"And done a fantastic job at it too," Mrs. Kim added.

"Thank you, dear. And your mother has been the maître d' at some of the finest restaurants in Colorado. We've always dreamed of starting our own hotel."

"And you know how much we enjoy skiing," Mrs. Kim added.

"So when the Wharton Mansion was posted for sale yesterday and for such a steal, it seemed like the perfect opportunity to realize our dream," Mr. Kim said.

"You like skiing too, Maggie," Mrs. Kim pointed out.

"Yeah, but I don't need it to be my life—"

"What life?" Simon teased her again.

"Simon, leave your sister alone," Mr. Kim scolded.

"Gladly," Simon said. He popped his earbuds in. His

dark-brown hair flopped around as he bobbed his head to the music.

Maggie peered back out the window. By now the multitude of lights had given way to occasional but bright neon strip malls illuminating the darkness. The earlier snow flurries had accelerated into a steadier curtain of white, descending in the night sky, visible in the headlights of the oncoming traffic.

"Your mother and I will be able to run the hotel, lodge, and ski slopes, all while living in a beautiful mountain setting," Mr. Kim said. "It really sounded perfect from the description the realtor gave us when we grabbed the keys from her office this morning."

"What a nice woman Nancy McGee is," Mrs. Kim continued. "She also told us that the previous owner of the house, who was known to everyone as Old Man Wharton, died about a year ago. She said that no one has even been inside the house since then, because several distant cousins of the late owner have been battling over the will. They finally settled the estate just two days ago, and want to sell the mansion immediately. So Nancy posted the listing before she had even gotten a chance to clean it up."

"We'll be the first ones to see it!" Mr. Kim said enthusiastically.

"What about neighbors?" Maggie asked. "Are there any?"

"Sure!" Mr. Kim replied.

"Like five miles away?"

"No!" Mr. Kim cried, as if Maggie had just said the most ridiculous thing in the world. "More like three miles."

"Oh, that's a lot better," Maggie said sarcastically.

"I'll come and visit," Sophie said, trying to make her friend feel better. "After all, BFFs are BFFs."

"I know," Maggie said and smiled. Sophie was trying so hard to cheer her up. "But you'll get to go home. To a real town. With real people. I'll be living full-time up in the middle of nowhere, with real bears."

Mrs. Kim turned to face Maggie. "Please just give this a chance. This is very important to your father and me. At least indulge us and take a look at the place before you decide it's going to be a living nightmare."

"Fine," Maggie said. Feeling satisfied, her mother turned around. Maggie slid even farther down into her seat. *A living nightmare. That's the perfect description for this. The only thing missing now is zombies.*

She stared out the window again. This time she saw long stretches of darkness broken only by the occasional house glowing invitingly like a warm oasis in the frozen rural landscape.

Simon looked over at his sister and saw that she had slipped into one of her rare quiet moods. He figured the time was right to broach what had been on his mind since the moment he had climbed into the car.

"So Mom, Dad, can I go skiing tomorrow?" he asked. "I threw my skis onto the roof rack before we left, and I have my helmet and equipment bag, so I've got what I need."

"I don't know, honey," Mrs. Kim replied. "From the pictures I saw online, the house is pretty dilapidated, and the slopes look like they haven't been groomed or maintained in quite some time. We might have a lot of work ahead of us before anyone can go skiing."

"Luckily, the mansion is so cheap that any amount of fixing up would still be worth it," Mr. Kim added.

"There's nothing to worry about, Mom," Simon said, fully prepared with his comeback. "I've skied lots of rough slopes before."

"Can we just wait until we see the place and then decide?" Mom asked.

"Sure," Simon replied, though his mind had been made up the moment he'd attached his skis to the rack.

The next few minutes passed in silence. The snowfall continued to pick up, and the *whish-whish, whish-whish* of the windshield wipers lulled everyone into a deep quiet.

"Maybe there's something on the radio," Mrs. Kim said finally when she grew uncomfortable with the silence that had overtaken the car.

As she scrolled through the dial, country music blared from the speakers, followed by pop, classical, and talk. Unsatisfied with any of the offerings, Mrs. Kim kept pushing the scan button, hoping to land on something she liked.

Maggie turned to Sophie and leaned in close.

"Dilapidated?" she whispered under the clatter of the radio. "They didn't mention that detail before."

"Maybe it won't be that bad," Sophie said hopefully.

But Maggie was nervous. "And what about school? If my parents need to move right away to start getting set up for next year, then that would mean leaving school before the spring play and before softball season and before the yearbook committee starts to work on this year's book. Starting a new school in the middle of the year is the worst!"

"Well, the good news is that they'll probably have all that stuff at your new school."

The phrase "your new school" sent shudders down Maggie's spine. It brought home the depth of what this move would mean. If this crazy plan actually came to pass, every part of Maggie's life would completely change.

"Great," Maggie moaned quietly to Sophie. "They'll probably do a fully staged production of *She'll Be Comin' 'Round the Mountain: The Musical*. And who will I play softball against, a team of chipmunks? And their yearbook is probably black and white and one page long."

"Come on, Mags," Sophie said. "You know that stuff isn't true."

"I know, I know," Maggie admitted. "It's just that I'm not going to know anybody, and I'll be the weird kid from suburbia."

"You're already the weird kid from suburbia," Simon chimed in.

"Seriously, Simon?" Maggie gave her brother a look.

"What, honey?" Mrs. Kim said from the front seat. This last bit of conversation had penetrated through the blaring of the radio.

"Nothing, Mom. Nothing."

Maggie looked out the window again. This time she could barely see past the heavy snow swirling around outside.

The last leg of the trip passed in complete silence. Maggie felt the car slow down.

"Are we here?" she asked.

"Almost," Mr. Kim said. "We're in the closest town. It's called Piney Hill, population three hundred."

Maggie sat up and looked outside. Most of the buildings were shuttered. Those that weren't were dark and already closed for the night. All except one.

"Wait. This is the town?" she cried in disbelief. "Where's the supermarket? Where's the shoe store? Where's—"

"There's our dinner!" Mr. Kim interrupted.

He pointed out the front windshield. Just ahead, a single building appeared open. Light poured from its windows. A blinking neon sign flickered above the front door. It stayed lit long enough for Maggie to read CLEM'S CHINESE KITCHEN.

"Takeout!" Mr. Kim said. "See, Mags. Just like home."

He pulled up to the entrance and opened his door. Blowing snow swirled into the car. "I'll be right back."

As Maggie waited for her dad to return with dinner, her mind raced through all the horrors she anticipated about her new life. No friends, having to start over at school, a house with guests coming and going all the time. A few minutes later her dad returned with a big plastic bag.

"Okay, I got egg rolls for everyone, spareribs, beef and broccoli, veggie lo mein, all your faves, Mags," Mr. Kim said. "And by the way, Clem says hi. Says you'll love his Chinese food."

Maggie couldn't help but smile a little. "Thanks, Dad." Her dad was trying, after all. And sometimes, his unshakable optimism could actually be contagious.

"That's the spirit," said Mr. Kim as he pulled the car away from the curb and continued down Main Street. At the edge of the little town, he turned right and started slowly up a steep hill.

"Just fifteen more minutes up this hill and we're there!" he said, his excitement growing.

Slipping and sliding a bit on the icy hill, the car finally made it to a level plateau in the road. A few seconds later an opening in the trees appeared on the left. Mr. Kim turned and the car rumbled up the long, twisting driveway.

Ahead Maggie spotted a sprawling mansion. She couldn't believe her eyes.

"It's just what they call a fixer-upper," Mr. Kim said enthusiastically, anticipating everyone's reaction.

"It should be called a tear-it-downer!" Maggie exclaimed.

"Now, Maggie. I—"

"Wait," Maggie interrupted, pointing to one of the windows on the first floor. Through the heavy snow she could just make out the face of an old man. He was staring down at the driveway, glaring directly at their car. The light from the room he was in illuminated his whole appearance, making him look unnaturally bright.

"There's someone already in the house!" Maggie cried.

# CHAPTER 2

"Where?" Sophie asked, leaning forward.

"Right there!" Maggie shouted, pointing again at a group of windows on the first floor of the house. She pulled her cell phone out of her bag, aimed it toward the house, and quickly snapped a picture.

"I don't see anything, honey," Mrs. Kim said, squinting through the snow at the house.

Maggie stared straight ahead. The man she had seen was gone. The room that had been lit was dark.

"I don't know where he went, but I *did* see him," she exclaimed.

"See who?" Simon asked, removing his earbuds, finally deciding to pay attention to his panicked sister.

"I have no idea," Maggie replied. "I just know I saw

a face. It kinda looked like an old man. Are we sure it's safe to go into this house?"

"Must have been the light from our headlights reflecting in the window," Mr. Kim said. "It was just a trick of the light."

"This was no trick. It was a face!"

That was when Maggie remembered the picture she'd just taken.

"Look at this!" she cried.

She scrolled to the picture of the house. The photo was blurry and dark, but she could definitely see something in the window.

"There!" she said triumphantly, holding out her phone for everyone to see. "There he is!"

Simon and Sophie leaned in to get a good look.

"I don't see a face," Simon said.

"I don't either, Mags," Sophie agreed. "Maybe it's a reflection that sort of looks like a face, but it really could be anything."

Maggie leaned forward into the front seat. "Here, look," she said, holding the phone out so her parents could see.

"I agree with Sophie, honey," Mrs. Kim said. "I

see something there, but it looks to me like headlights reflecting off the window, creating a strange shape."

"It's probably just your imagination, honey," Mr. Kim said, glancing briefly at the photo. "The realtor said that no one has entered this house for a year, and we have the only key. Besides, the alarm system has been on the entire year, and it was never deactivated or set off. The realtor made a point of assuring us of that this morning."

Maggie felt a chill race through her body. *What if there is someone hiding in the house?* she wondered. *Someone waiting to get us in the middle of the night?* A wave of fear washed over her, and she sank back into her seat.

Mr. Kim pulled the car up to the front door and shut off the engine.

"Welcome to the Wharton Mansion, everybody," he said. "Or should I call it the future Piney Hill Ski Resort?"

"Don't . . . please," Maggie said as she stepped from the car and threw her backpack over her shoulder. Her sneakers sank into a snowdrift, soaking her feet. Snow continued to fall as she looked up at the mansion and wiggled her cold, wet toes.

Many windows were cracked. Ancient shutters twisted in the wind, making a squealing, creaking sound that penetrated the stillness of the night.

"Just a few repairs and this place will look like new," Mr. Kim said, looking up. "Well, let's get inside. The real estate agent said that we should probably be able to get the furnace running. The place is going to be chilly after being empty for so long."

Mr. Kim led his family to the front door. "This is it," he said to his wife, kissing her gently on the cheek. "The beginning of a dream come true."

He punched in the code for the alarm that was next to the doorbell and then put the key in the lock. He grabbed the knob on the front door and turned it. The knob snapped off in his hand with a metallic crunch. He pushed the door and it swung open, creaking and moaning as it moved.

"Well, we'll have to get that fixed," Mr. Kim said, looking down at the doorknob in his hand. "Come on in, everyone."

And with that, he entered the house. He walked down the hallway and flipped a light switch. A dusty crystal chandelier blazed to life. The bulbs illuminated long, stringy cobwebs dangling from the crystals.

"At least the power works," he said as the others followed him into the dining room. "Simon, girls, just put your bags down over there. We'll check out the bedrooms after we eat. Now, who's hungry?"

Mr. Kim rubbed his hands together excitedly, then carried the bag of takeout over to a long table covered by a sheet.

"Let me get that," Mrs. Kim said, grabbing a corner of the sheet and pulling it off. A cloud of dust filled the dining room.

"Gross!" Simon choked out between coughs.

"I brought some cleaning supplies, since we didn't know what shape the place would be in," Mrs. Kim said, pulling furniture polish and some rags from a bag she had brought along. "I'll have that table ready in no time."

"I'll see if I can get the furnace running while you put out our delicious Chinese feast," Mr. Kim said.

"Made by my new friend, Clem," said Maggie.

"Mags, Sophie, why don't you give me a hand downstairs with the furnace?" Mr. Kim continued. "Simon, help your mother set the table."

"You're kidding, right?" Simon asked.

"What?" Mr. Kim asked, spreading his arms wide. "Only boys should help with the furnace and only girls should set the table? This is the twenty-first century, Simon."

Maggie and Sophie followed Mr. Kim to the staircase leading down to the cellar. He paused at the top of the stairs.

"Let me just flip this light on," he said, hitting a switch.

Nothing happened.

Mr. Kim flipped the switch up and down a few more times, but had no luck. "Maggie, can you go get a flashlight from my bag of tools?" he asked.

"Sure," Maggie replied. She headed back into the dining room, where all the bags had been dropped.

"Done already?" Mrs. Kim asked.

"Nah, Dad needs a flashlight," Maggie explained.

She knelt down and pulled open the heavy canvas bag in which her dad carried his tools. Back home, it lived in the garage and sat on what passed for a workbench. Before they left for this weekend, he had tossed it into the car, just in case.

Rummaging past screwdrivers of every size, several hammers, rolls of duct tape, and a few unidentifiable objects, Maggie found a flashlight. She snatched it up, snapped the bag shut, and returned to the top of the cellar stairs, where she handed it to her father.

"Here we go," he said, aiming the beam down the old wooden stairs. He started down, followed by Maggie, then Sophie.

Maggie felt the staircase shift and creak with each step.

"I don't think these stairs are safe," she said.

"Sure they are," her dad replied. "This place hasn't been empty for *that* long. Just hold on to the railing."

Maggie reached out and grabbed the thin wooden railing that ran down the length of the staircase, and her hand plunged into a sticky mixture of dust and cobwebs.

"Yuck," she said in disgust, wiping her hand on the wall, only to disturb a spider, which scurried away in annoyance.

The trio reached the bottom of the stairs and followed Mr. Kim's flashlight beam, careful to bend low to avoid getting whacked in the head by the maze of metal ductwork. They came to a hulking metal structure.

"Looks like a furnace to me," Mr. Kim said as he set the gas valve to "pilot" and handed the flashlight to Sophie. "Just shine the beam down near the bottom. I'll get the pilot light going."

"What's my job?" Maggie asked, pretending to be interested.

"You watch out for critters," Mr. Kim said, smiling.

"C-critters?" Maggie stammered. "You mean, like animals? Here in the house?" She glanced left, then right, certain she would spot a ferocious beast ready to spring at her. Fear welled up inside her once again. Between the man she had seen in the window and the possibility of wild animals in the cellar, her nerves were totally on edge.

Mr. Kim knelt at the bottom of the furnace and pulled out a box of long matches. "Let's see. Boy, I haven't seen a furnace like this in . . . well, ever, actually. That pilot light has to be around here somewhere. You know, when I was in college, I—"

A sudden clatter startled Maggie. The sound moved across the cellar toward them, growing louder and louder.

"Dad, someone's down here!" she cried.

Sophie swung the flashlight beam in the direction of the sound. A black cat squinted into the light.

"Critters," Mr. Kim said. "Told ya."

Maggie shuddered, partly from the adrenaline that was coursing through her veins, and partly from being shocked by the thought of sharing her possible new home with stray animals.

"Got it!" Mr. Kim exclaimed as the pilot light caught and a ring of flame raced around the furnace's burner. "There. It should be toasty in here in no time. Come on. Let's go eat!"

As she followed Sophie and her dad up the cellar stairs, Maggie wondered what other surprises awaited them in this house.

In the dining room, Mrs. Kim had done her best to make their first meal in what she hoped would be their new home special. She had sprayed and wiped down the long wooden table with furniture polish. Then she placed a candelabra containing six white candles on the center of the table. When the rest of her family returned from the cellar, she lit all six.

"Grandma's fine china," Mrs. Kim said as Simon pulled a stack of paper plates from the take-out bag and set one at each chair.

Maggie laughed softly. "She says that every time we use paper plates," she said to Sophie.

The containers of food and cans of soda came out next.

"Okay, everybody," Mr. Kim announced, rubbing his palms together. "Dig in!"

Maggie hadn't realized just how hungry she was. Even though the Chinese food was getting cold, it tasted pretty good. The room was silent as everyone shoved forkfuls of food into their mouths.

Mr. Kim raised his soda can. "To our first meal in the Piney Hill Ski Resort," he announced, offering a toast. "May we look back on this weekend in years to come and remember how this great adventure began."

Everybody raised their own can and sipped their soda.

"Can we look back on how it ended instead?" Maggie asked and then a forced smile.

"All right, Maggie. Time for a little positivity," Mrs. Kim said. "I'm hoping that you will come to think of this place as home."

"Well, maybe," Maggie said. "Once the intruders and the animals all leave."

"With the alarm system and the fact that we have the only key, I'm a hundred percent sure the house is empty, but why don't you check it out?" Mr. Kim suggested.

Sophie smiled. "Come on, Mags. We can make it an adventure."

Maggie finished chewing her bite of lo mein and then reluctantly slid her chair back and got up.

"Have fun exploring," Mrs. Kim said. "I think once you get to know it, you'll love this place, Maggie. And be careful. No one has been in this house for a while."

"Yeah, except Maggie's man in the window might be lurking in the shadows! Mwa-aaaa!" Simon teased, curling his hands into claws and making a scary face.

"That's not what I meant, Simon," Mrs. Kim said quickly. "Just be sure there aren't any holes in the floor or falling plaster or other dangerous things. Now go have a good time."

Maggie said nothing as she followed Sophie out of the dining room.

"But be careful!" Mrs. Kim repeated.

The two friends entered a long hallway.

"It sure is a big old house," Sophie said. "You could get lost in here."

"Just what I want to do," Maggie said, turning to look at the peeling old wallpaper that covered the hallway. "Get lost in my own house."

Then she stopped in her tracks.

"Did I just say that? 'My own house.'"

"I won't tell a soul," Sophie said, smiling.

Maggie started walking again to see where the hallway led and got a face full of cobwebs that had been hanging from the ceiling, waiting for a victim.

"Not again!" Maggie cried, clawing at her face to pull the sticky, filthy strands from her eyes and nose.

"Gotta watch where you're going, Mags," Sophie offered.

"Yeah, thanks."

They followed the hallway as it curved to the left. The light from the one working bulb in the ceiling grew dimmer as they walked. At the end of the hallway, they came to a door. Maggie stopped short.

"Well, go ahead and open it," said Sophie. "It's not going to bite you."

"What if the old man I saw is inside?" Maggie asked, genuinely afraid.

"Go ahead, Mags. It'll be okay. I promise."

Maggie turned the knob and pushed the door open, its rusty hinges complaining as it swung inward.

Stepping into the room, she flipped the light switch, but nothing happened.

"I'll go back and get the flashlight," said Sophie. She

turned and headed back down the hallway.

Maggie stepped farther into the room and noticed a dull light flickering. It was coming from a far corner in the back of the room.

*What's that?* she wondered.

Crossing the room slowly, squinting in the soft light, she saw floor-to-ceiling bookcases stacked with musty old volumes. A round woven rug sat in the middle of the room, surrounded by chairs and standing floor lamps. All this was difficult to see by the weak light that played around the room.

Then she stopped and stared.

"How is that possible?" she said aloud to no one, pointing to the source of the light.

In a far corner of the room, on a small round table, a single lit white candle sat in an old metal candlestick. Its flame danced and its flickering light reflected on the ceiling above.

"Who's here?" Maggie yelled out into the empty room.

# CHAPTER 3

Maggie dashed from the room as fast as she could. Turning the corner of the hallway, she almost crashed into Sophie, who was on her way back with a flashlight.

"Soph, hurry!" Maggie cried.

"Mags, you're white as a ghost. What happened?"

"Just come with me. You need to see this. Now!"

Maggie grabbed Sophie's hand and practically dragged her down the hallway to the library.

"Let me turn the flashlight on so I can see what you want to show me," Sophie said as they hurried inside.

"No, no flashlight," Maggie replied.

"Then how are we going to see where we're going?"

It was then that Maggie realized the flickering was gone. The room was completely dark, except for the light seeping in from the hallway.

She snatched the flashlight from Sophie's hand and turned it on. Crossing the room quickly, she trained the light on the small round table in the corner. The single white candle was unlit.

"Sophie, I swear that this candle was lit a moment ago. Whoever lit it must have blown it out when I went to get you. That means that there was someone in this room!"

"No, Mags, wait," Sophie said, reaching out and aiming the flashlight beam at the candle. "Look at the wick. It's white, still coated with wax. It's not burnt at all. This candle has never been lit."

Maggie stared at the candle and saw that Sophie was right. "How can that be?"

"Could you have imagined it?" asked Sophie.

"Don't you start now with the 'it's only your imagination' routine," Maggie shot back. "It's bad enough when my mom does it."

Maggie sighed. This whole thing was getting creepier by the second.

"I have to tell my parents about this. I truly believe that there is someone here in the house with us. They need to know."

"Let's go," Sophie said, seeing how upset her friend was. The two girls returned to the dining room.

"Back so soon?" Mr. Kim asked. "All done exploring?"

"Dad, there is most definitely someone in the house with us," Maggie said.

Mr. Kim looked right at his daughter and got up.

"Did you actually see someone?" he asked. "Where?"

"Well, not exactly," Maggie explained. "I walked into a room and found a lit candle. I know that none of us lit the candle, unless Simon pulled some kind of prank."

"It wasn't me," Simon shot back. "I've been here the whole time, helping Mom clean up."

"Okay, then. Someone must have lit that candle, right? Oh, and then they blew it out and replaced it with another candle."

"I'm not following you, honey," Mrs. Kim said from the kitchen.

"Come on, Maggie," Mr. Kim said, grabbing his flashlight. "I'll take a walk around the house with you. If there actually is someone here, we'll find him."

Maggie wasn't sure her dad believed her, but she was relieved and pleased that he wanted to at least go with her to check out her story.

Sophie tagged along as Maggie and Mr. Kim headed back down the hallway.

"This house really does need some work," Mr. Kim said, looking around at the peeling plaster and dangling cobwebs.

They reached the door at the end of the hallway.

"Okay, Dad, put on the flashlight," Maggie said. "The bulb in this room isn't working."

Mr. Kim switched on the light, and Maggie led the way into the room.

The flashlight beam washed over the bookshelves and chairs in the room.

"Looks like a study or a library," Mr. Kim commented.

"That's what we thought," Sophie said.

"Hello? Anybody in here?" Mr. Kim called out.

He led the girls into the room. Guided by his flashlight, they walked around the edge of the room until they came to the table with the candle.

"Is this it?" Mr. Kim asked Maggie.

"Yeah," she replied, looking back over her shoulder, half expecting someone to jump out from behind a chair.

Mr. Kim aimed his light at the candle. "This candle's never been lit, Maggie," he said.

"I know, Dad," Maggie said, worried that maybe this tour of the house wasn't such a good idea after all. "But I swear that I saw a lit candle. Then, in the time it took me to go get Sophie, that lit candle was switched for this one. I can't explain how. I just know what I saw."

"Well, there's nothing odd in this room," Mr. Kim said, heading back to the door. "Let's keep searching the house."

With Maggie's father leading the way, the trio wandered from room to room. Each door they came to, they opened. Most of the doors opened into dark, empty rooms, filled with dust and cobwebs but no furniture, and certainly no people lurking in the shadows. After they were finished searching the first floor, Mr. Kim went off by himself and did a quick check of the second floor and attic as well.

"I've been through the entire house and didn't see anyone or any sign of anyone, Maggie," he said as he returned to the dining room.

Maggie let out a big sigh of relief. She didn't have an explanation for what she had seen, but she couldn't deny that it didn't seem like anyone could be in the house. "All right, then, I'm going to go to bed."

"Good night, honey," Mrs. Kim said. "Sleep tight."

"Good night," Maggie said, and then she gave each of her parents a hug. "And thanks for reassuring me, Dad."

"You betcha!" Mr. Kim said. "Sleep well."

Maggie and Sophie grabbed their bags and headed up the staircase that led to the second floor. The stairs were sagging and well-worn, but Maggie could see that this had once been the grand staircase of a magnificent mansion. At the top of the stairs, she and Sophie stepped into a wide hallway that led to a series of doors.

"Bedrooms, I guess," Maggie said.

"Let's find out," Sophie said, flinging open the first door she came to.

Someone jumped out, right at the girls, crashing to the floor at their feet.

"Ahh!" they both screamed, stumbling backward and landing on top of each other. Looking down, they saw that what had leaped out at them was only an old doll. Peering into the closet, they saw a mountain of toys and children's clothing that had been piled up against the door.

"I feel dumb," Maggie said as she and Sophie climbed back to their feet.

"Well, that door obviously hasn't been opened in a really long time," Sophie said, picking up the doll, tossing it back into the closet, and slamming the door.

"Lucky us, huh?" Maggie said, brushing herself off.

"Girls, are you all right?" Mrs. Kim called from downstairs.

"Fine, Mom!" Maggie yelled back.

"I heard a scream," Mrs. Kim said.

"Everything's okay, Mom. Don't worry. We're going to sleep."

"All right. Good night, girls."

"Good night, Mrs. Kim," Sophie called down.

Continuing down the hall, they picked another door, swung it open, and jumped back—just in case. This time, nothing sprang out. They flipped on the light and stepped into a large bedroom with two beds.

Long, silk, flower-printed draperies hung from a bowed-out picture window and flowed down to the floor. Each bed had a canopy with matching fabric. Two oak dressers stood majestically on wooden floorboards that were scuffed from decades of use.

"Ohh," Sophie cooed. "Pretty. I want that bed!"

She dropped her suitcase on the floor and flopped onto a bed. It creaked as the mattress bounced up and down and finally came to rest.

"I didn't realize how tired I was," Sophie said. "I guess driving out to the middle of nowhere and eating cold Chinese food takes a lot out of a girl."

"What do you think the chances of getting cell service here are?" Maggie asked, sitting on her bed and pulling out her cell phone.

"Slim to none gets my vote," Sophie replied, glancing at her own phone.

"Nothing. Not even a hint of a bar," Maggie said.

"Ooh, cut off from civilization!" Sophie said in a creepy-sounding voice. "Adds to the fun."

"Now you're starting to sound like my dad!" Maggie said, laughing.

"Your dad is a pretty cool guy, you know, walking around the house with us to make you feel better," Sophie pointed out.

"Yeah, I know," Maggie admitted. "I just wish he wasn't so gung-ho about buying this place."

She grabbed her bag and headed down the hallway toward the bathroom. She turned on the faucet. It squealed in protest, then spat out brown water.

"Eww!" she cried, stepping back. "Maybe I won't brush my teeth."

But in a few seconds the water started running clear, and Maggie braved brushing her teeth.

*Must have just needed a minute to get back to normal,* Maggie thought, swishing a mouthful around before spitting it into the sink.

After both girls finished getting ready for bed, Maggie turned off the light and they slipped under their covers.

"Do you think your parents are really going to go through with all this?" Sophie asked in the darkness and then yawned.

"I hope not," Maggie replied. She was feeling a little better than she had when they arrived, but she wondered how she would actually deal with the move, if it happened. All the fears she had about living way up in the isolated mountains and leaving everything and everyone she knew filled her with anxiety. "But they do seem determined to do this. I can only hope something makes them change their minds."

"Maybe we can check out the ski slopes tomorrow," Sophie offered. "That would be fun."

"Maybe," Maggie said, trying hard not to sound so negative all the time. "Anyway, thanks for coming with me, Soph. At least I have someone to talk to. I don't know what I'd do if the only one I could confide in was Simon. He's about as helpful to talk to as this canopy. And come to think of it, I might get more intelligent answers from the canopy."

Sophie didn't reply.

"Soph?"

Maggie heard gentle snores coming from the other bed. She smiled. "I guess you really *were* tired," she said softly. Then she turned onto her back and stared up into the darkness.

Her mind raced, searching for some reason to feel positive about this potential move. She struggled to find one. *What if nobody likes me at my new school? What if I'll always be the new kid? What if—*

A sudden noise startled Maggie. She listened closely and heard what sounded like a voice.

"Shhh . . ." She heard a soft whisper.

"Soph, is that you?"

But Maggie was greeted only by Sophie's soft breathing.

"Shhh . . ." Maggie heard the whisper again, this time a little louder, coming from just outside the bedroom door.

"If Simon is playing some kind of joke on me . . . ," said Maggie, tossing off the covers, throwing on her slippers, and tiptoeing quietly toward the bedroom door.

Grasping the brass knob, she turned it and flung the door open.

No one was there.

Switching on a flashlight, Maggie headed for the stairs.

"Follow me . . ." The voice came again, this time from the bottom of the stairs.

Stepping softly but quickly down the stairs, Maggie swept the flashlight beam all around. The downstairs was dark. Everyone else had gone to bed. She was alone, and she was getting scared all over again.

"Over here," she heard. She pointed her flashlight toward the front door, and the beam illuminated a face. *The* face. The face of the man she had seen in the window when she first arrived. Deep creases ran the length of his leathery, wrinkled face. Thin wisps of white hair dangled randomly from his mostly bald head.

"Who are you?" Maggie whispered tensely.

"Shhh . . . ," the old man whispered again, placing a single bony, gnarled finger to his lips. Then he opened the front door and stepped outside.

Fighting every instinct to do the opposite, Maggie followed the man to the front door and stepped out into the night.

She could barely see through a swirling wall of snow and wind that assaulted her, shoving her back against the closed door. Shining her flashlight into the blinding whiteness, hoping to catch a glimpse of the man, she saw only the flashlight beam reflected back into her eyes.

"Where are you?" Maggie demanded. "Show yourself and tell me what you want!"

Fear mounted inside her. She now knew for certain that an old man had been hiding in the house. And now he had lured her outside. But for what purpose?

"I'm not afraid of you!" Maggie shouted, lying. Her hand trembled, the flashlight beam shaking in the swirling snow.

Again she got no answer.

*Maybe I can go back inside and lock him out,* she thought.

She grabbed the doorknob, only to discover that the front door had locked behind her. She was trapped outside in a raging blizzard with a man who seemed to be able to appear and disappear at will!

# CHAPTER 4

Maggie's eyes flew open, and she clutched the covers. As her eyes adjusted to the dim light, she looked around the cozy room.

*It was just a dream!* she thought gleefully. *Time to go back to sleep. There was no old man in the house. I didn't get locked outside. Mom and Dad were right. This is all in my imagination.*

But try as she might, Maggie could not fall back to sleep. Every time she closed her eyes, she saw the face of the man from her dream.

After about half an hour, she slipped quietly from bed, grabbed a flashlight, and headed downstairs. Glancing at a grandfather clock in the hallway, she saw that it was three in the morning . . . if the clock was still right, that is.

Retracing her steps from that evening down the long,

cobweb-filled hallway, Maggie arrived at the room where she had seen the lit candle. Opening the door slowly, she shone her flashlight into the room, then stepped in.

Everything looked exactly as it had when she had last been in there. Crossing the room, Maggie came to the table where the candle still sat. Its wick was still pristine and never used, just as it had been when Sophie and her dad saw it.

"I really don't think I was dreaming when I saw the lit candle," she mumbled to herself. "There has to be a logical explanation."

Maggie swept the flashlight beam across the many shelves of books, running floor to ceiling, across the entire room—all except for one wall. The wall nearest the small table, was made up of a series of wooden panels and no shelves.

Maggie explored the seams between sections of the paneled wall. She ran her hand along the smooth but dusty panels.

*I've watched too many mystery movies,* she thought, searching for some clue. *I'm not sure what I'm expecting here.*

Her fingers came to rest on a raised square corner of a panel. As she started to move her hand away, she felt the square move slightly. Gripping it tightly, she rotated the square. It turned smoothly, like a doorknob.

The panel above the square knob slid open with the grinding, scraping sound of old, dry wood moving along a rusty metal track.

"Bingo!" she cried. "A secret passage. I knew it!"

With her flashlight leading the way, Maggie stepped through the opening. She found herself in a narrow passageway, so constricted that she had to turn sideways to continue. After a few yards, the passageway took a sharp right turn, then ended abruptly at a wall. Hanging on the wall was a portrait of a young man done in oil, labeled SAMUEL WHARTON.

"Could that be Old Man Wharton?" Maggie wondered aloud. "The guy who owned the house and died last year?"

She peered closely at the face in the painting. It looked similar to, but not quite the same as, the face she had seen in the window and the face of the man who'd terrified her in the dream she'd just had.

Maggie reached up and touched the picture frame. It shifted slightly to the right—and the wall it was hanging on slid open, revealing the other end of the secret passage. It was a secret passage within a secret passage!

She stepped through the opening and found herself in a small bedroom, containing a single bed, a narrow dresser, and one standing floor lamp. Additional portraits hung on the wall, all of the same subject.

"Someone sure was obsessed with this Samuel guy," she said softly, feeling for some reason that it was inappropriate to speak too loudly in this room. It almost felt like a shrine, a place that was very special to someone.

Scattered beneath the portraits were old, broken pieces of ski equipment. Long wooden skis, leather straps for boots, primitive goggles.

Fear suddenly gripped her. *Whoever lit the candle, then replaced it with the new one, must have used this passageway! He could be in this room right now!* she thought. Maggie spun around quickly, fully expecting to see someone standing behind her.

She was alone.

Retracing her steps, she stepped back into the passageway. She straightened out the picture, and the wall slid closed. Walking sideways back through the narrow passage, she stepped through the open panel and out into the library. She twisted the square wooden knob, and the second panel slid shut.

"So that's how he did it," she said once she was back in the library. "He hid in that secret room, then snuck in and switched the candles."

*But who?* Maggie wondered. *Old Man Wharton is dead. Who is in this house with us?*

Hurrying back to her room, she quietly entered, locked the door, and slipped back into bed.

Maggie tossed and turned until nearly dawn, then slept fitfully and for just a short while before the morning sun poured into her window, waking her up. Glancing over to the other bed, she saw that Sophie was already up and out of the room.

Maggie rolled out of bed, threw on her clothes, and slouched down the stairs to the kitchen. She discovered that her mom had already driven to the small market in Piney Hill and picked up food for breakfast.

Bacon sizzled in a metal skillet, making the musty old house smell like a real home. A big bowl of eggs sat ready to be dropped into a pan to be scrambled. An electric coffeepot percolated enthusiastically on the counter.

"Good morning, Sleeping Beauty," Mr. Kim teased his daughter. "Planning to sleep all day?"

"Ha-ha, Dad," Maggie said, groaning. "That's so funny I forgot to laugh."

"Weak, Mags," Simon said, shoving a piece of toast into his mouth. "The last time I heard that one I nearly fell off my dinosaur."

"Who's ready for eggs?" Mrs. Kim interrupted.

"Right here," Simon said, holding out his plate.

"Thanks, Mrs. Kim," Sophie said, getting up to help serve the breakfast as Mrs. Kim went back to scrambling more eggs.

"So, um, I had an interesting night," Maggie began once everyone was seated around the table. "I was up most of the night, investigating the house."

"Ooh, investigating," Simon echoed, unable to stifle a giggle. "What exactly were you investigating, Sherlock? How many cobwebs and dead bugs are in this house?"

Maggie ignored him. "I couldn't sleep, and I was still curious about that candle. I know I saw it burning, but then when we all looked again, it had been replaced."

Maggie's parents exchanged a look.

"Do you think I'm making this up?" she asked indignantly.

"First the man in the window, now a mysterious

candle that lights itself and then replaces itself," Mrs. Kim said. "I don't know whether it's your imagination or if you're making stuff up to try to scare us. I'm beginning to think you'd try to find any excuse to convince us not to live here."

"That is not true!" Maggie insisted. She might not want to move here, but she wasn't a liar.

"Well, all you did the whole car ride up here was complain," Mrs. Kim continued. "You made a point of telling us all the reasons you didn't want to live here, despite the fact that you had never even seen the place. How can we believe that you're willing to give it a fair chance?"

"And you're the only one who has seen anything," added Simon.

Maggie scowled at him. It was just like Simon to take her parents' side, especially when there was something he wanted—and Simon usually just wanted to ski.

"You know what? Just forget it," Maggie grumbled. She ate her eggs in silence, then got up and left the table. Sophie followed.

"Your father and I are going outside to tour the grounds," Mrs. Kim said. "Would you girls like to come?"

"Not really," Maggie replied sullenly.

"I'll go," Simon said, jumping up from the table, grabbing his empty plate, and heading to the kitchen. "I want to check out those slopes."

"Great!" said Mr. Kim. "But no skiing today. We need to make sure it's safe first."

As her parents and brother bundled up to head outside, Maggie led Sophie down the hallway they had explored the previous day.

She stopped suddenly and turned to her best friend.

"You know I'm not making all this up, right, Soph?" Maggie asked. "I mean, yes, I really don't want to leave home and move here, but I'm not so selfish that I would make up crazy, impossible stories that no one would believe anyway, just to stop my parents from buying this house."

"I know that, Mags," Sophie said, reaching out and squeezing her friend's hand. "And I know you. You are not a liar. I'm as in the dark about all this as you are."

"Thanks, Soph." Maggie paused and then continued. Even if her parents didn't want to listen to her, she had to tell someone about what happened. "So, I had this really weird dream last night. It was so real. I was sure I was awake."

"What happened?"

"It started in the room we slept in last night. You were asleep. I was so wired I couldn't fall asleep. My mind was racing. Next thing I knew, I heard a whispered voice saying 'shh.'

"So I got out of bed and followed the voice downstairs. I saw an old man—the same old man I saw in the window when we arrived here. He opened the front door and stepped outside. I followed him out into a blizzard. I was superscared.

"I couldn't see a thing, so I decided to come back in, but the door was locked and I was stuck outside. That's when I woke up."

"Sounds really scary, Mags," Sophie said as they reached the library door at the end of the hall.

"But what happened after I woke up was even scarier," Maggie said. "That's what I need to show you. Come on."

She opened the door, and the two friends stepped into the library for the first time in the daylight. They saw a serious-looking room of dark wooden shelves filled with dust-covered books. Plushy upholstered chairs sat in each corner accompanied by a stained-glass floor lamp.

Maggie imagined spending a rainy Saturday afternoon curled up in one of those chairs with a good book and got a warm feeling for the first time since she'd arrived. Then she remembered all that had been going on since last night, and the warm feeling was replaced by the ever-more-familiar knot in her stomach.

"So last night, after I woke up, I came back to this room," she continued. "I knew what I saw with that candle, and I knew there had to be a logical explanation. I found it right there."

Maggie led Sophie over to the wood panel on the far wall. She grabbed the square wooden knob.

"A secret passageway leading to a hidden room!"

"No way!" said Sophie.

"Way! Watch."

Maggie tried to turn the knob, which had moved so easily during the night. But this time, the knob didn't budge.

"Wait a minute," she said, now gripping the knob with both hands. Again, it stood firm. "I swear, Soph, this knob turned last night. Then that panel slid open, and I walked down a secret passageway."

"Maybe you were still dreaming?" Sophie suggested. "You said the dream about being trapped outside felt so real. Maybe you didn't wake up and get out of bed.

Maybe you only dreamed that you did."

Maggie searched her memory, replaying the events of the dream and what had followed once she woke up— or at least, thought she woke up. Could the whole thing have been a dream?

"Why don't we check out the rest of the house, Mags?" Sophie asked, seeing her friend struggling to figure out what had happened to her.

Maggie fought off her disappointment. She didn't want to be mad at Sophie, her only ally in this miserable situation. And she realized that if the situation were reversed, she'd be having a lot of trouble believing Sophie.

"Sure," she said. "Let's go."

Heading back down the hallway, they stopped at a door on the left. "Good as any," Sophie said, throwing it open.

The two stepped into what appeared to be a small storage room. A startled spider scurried up its web, vanishing into a hole in the ceiling. Boxes and suitcases were piled in tall stacks. On a small table in the center of the room sat a pile of old photographs.

Maggie thumbed through the curling brown photos of people who'd lived long ago.

"Look at this one," she said, handing it to Sophie.

It was a shot of a man standing outside the Wharton Mansion holding a pair of skis.

"Is this the guy you saw in the window and in your dream?" Sophie asked, trying to be supportive of her friend.

"I'm not sure. It looks a bit like him, but . . ." Maggie suddenly recalled the paintings she had seen in the secret room. "No. It's not him. It's Samuel Wharton!"

"Who?" Sophie asked.

"I have no idea," Maggie replied. "But I saw portraits of him hanging in that secret room."

After flipping through the rest of the photos, none of which provided any insight into what had happened during the night, Maggie and Sophie continued their exploration of the house. Mostly they saw old rooms in disrepair, lots of cobwebs, a whole bunch of spiders, and a mouse or two.

None of this impressed Maggie or made her feel any happier about the prospect of living in this house. After a couple of hours more of exploring, Maggie heard the front door open, and an argument in progress entered the house.

"But you know I'm an excellent skier. I can take care of myself!"

"Simon, there are whiteout conditions out there," Maggie heard her dad say as she and Sophie joined the now-frozen members of her family. "That's why we came in."

"Hey, how was your outdoor tour?" Maggie asked, glad that she would not be the only one to argue with her parents this weekend.

"The grounds are really beautiful," Mrs. Kim said, shaking the snow off her down jacket and hood. "But the snow picked up a few minutes ago, and it's really nasty out there."

"How did the skiing look, Simon?" Sophie asked.

"Great. Big mountain. Perfect slopes. Everyone else in the world will get to ski here except me."

"Don't be so dramatic, Simon," Maggie said. "I'm sure you'll be able to ski when it's safe."

"But it's safe now," Simon whined. "I've skied in way worse weather."

"End of discussion," Mr. Kim said. "Now let's see if we can get that old fireplace going."

Mr. Kim managed to start a fire in the fireplace. The whole family gathered around and read, played board games, or napped for the remainder of the afternoon.

Dinner that night was very different from the cold Chinese food of the night before. Mrs. Kim made spaghetti and a vat of homemade sauce and a big salad. The fire blazed, and everyone dug into their dinners.

As delicious as the dinner was and as cozy as the house felt, Maggie couldn't help but feel scared. *What's going to happen tonight?* she wondered.

"Maybe I can go skiing tomorrow?" Simon asked during a lull in dinner conversation.

"We'll see," Mrs. Kim said. "Let's see what tomorrow brings weather-wise."

Maggie twirled a mass of spaghetti around her fork and shoveled it into her mouth. She was hungrier than she'd realized.

Then, looking up from her plate, Maggie saw a face peering around the corner from the hallway, staring into the dining room, looking right at her.

"Ahhhhh!" she shrieked in terror.

# CHAPTER 5

Maggie jumped up from the table, knocking her chair over backward. She pointed toward the hallway. Everyone in the dining room turned. This time, they all saw the face—the face of an old woman with careworn eyes sunk into deeply etched skin.

The woman stepped into the dining room.

"Excuse me," she said, looking as startled to see the Kims as they were to see her. "I didn't know that anyone was in the house."

"Who—who are you?" sputtered Mr. Kim.

"I am Karina Walcott," the old woman replied. Her heavy winter coat was covered in snow. "I have been the caretaker here at the Wharton Mansion for many years. I moved here from back east twenty years ago and worked for Mr. Wharton during that entire time, until he died that is. This is the first time I have been inside the house for a year."

"Why are you here now?" Mr. Kim asked.

"When Mr. Wharton died, there was a dispute over the will and this house among two of his distant cousins," Ms. Walcott explained. "I was rushed from the house before I had a chance to gather up the last of my possessions. The cousins changed the locks and refused to give me permission to enter until their dispute was settled.

"When this finally happened, only a few days ago, they agreed to give me a key so I could get my belongings and take them back to my apartment in Denver. So, that's why I'm here. And now, may I ask who *you* are?"

Mrs. Kim stepped forward. "We are the Kims. I'm Jeannie. This is my husband, Paul; our son, Simon; our daughter, Maggie; and Maggie's friend, Sophie. We're interested in buying the house."

"How do you do?" Ms. Walcott asked, nodding toward the group and smiling. Her eyes brightened slightly, her face softened. "I must say they didn't waste any time showing the house to potential buyers. I understand that the house was put on the market only a day or two ago."

"That's right," Mr. Kim said. "We were very lucky to be here the day this place became available."

"We love it," Mrs. Kim said enthusiastically. "It's got so much character."

"That's one way to put it," Maggie whispered to Sophie, who elbowed her friend to keep quiet. She stared at Ms. Walcott. "You said that you haven't been inside the house for a year?"

"That's right," Ms. Walcott replied.

"Do you mean until this very second or since last night, maybe?" Maggie persisted.

"What do you mean?" Ms. Walcott said defensively. "I just walked through the door a moment ago for the first time in a year. I did not expect to see anyone else here."

"Are you sure you weren't in the house last night?" Maggie asked, looking Ms. Walcott directly in the eye. "Perhaps lighting a candle or two?"

"Absolutely not," Ms. Walcott said indignantly. She was clearly a woman who was not used to having her word questioned by a child. "I believe I made myself perfectly clear."

"Yeah, well, someone has been in this house!" Maggie exclaimed. "I know it! I've seen the evidence."

"That's impossible," Ms. Walcott shot back. "There are only two keys, and we have both. All the other doors and windows are still locked, I presume?"

Mr. Kim nodded his head.

Maggie grew quiet, wondering whether she believed Ms. Walcott. It would explain a lot if she had been here last night. An awkward silence descended over the room.

"I'm sorry to be so rude," Ms. Walcott said suddenly, breaking the uncomfortable silence. "I didn't mean to interrupt your dinner. It's just that I wanted to get back here as soon as I could. This place means a great deal to me."

"It's totally cool," Simon spoke up. "Although I haven't been able to check out the skiing yet."

Ms. Walcott's face grew visibly grim. "Skiing?" she asked.

"That mountain's gonna make for some killer runs," Simon added.

"Young man, no one skis here," Ms. Walcott said. There was a sternness to her voice that had not been there before. "Not for many years, at any rate."

"Well, people will ski here now," Simon shot back defiantly. "We're buying this mansion and turning it into a ski resort."

Ms. Walcott's dark eyes narrowed, and her expression turned even graver, as if someone had just given her the worst news she had ever heard.

"Is something wrong, Ms. Walcott?" Mrs. Kim asked.

Ms. Walcott gazed into the distance, her thoughts clearly not in this moment. Then she spoke in a soft, even voice.

"This house was built in 1910 by Ernest Wharton, the patriarch of a successful banking family. They lived in a mansion in Denver, but Mr. Wharton wanted a country getaway. And he loved to ski. The family spent winters here. This mansion not only served to house Mr. Wharton's family, it allowed for their large extended family to come and go as they pleased. And it was also their private skiing grounds.

"But for the past forty years, the only person who lived here was the youngest Wharton son, the last member of the once large family, Jonas Wharton."

"Jonas?" Maggie said. "*He* was Old Man Wharton? Then who's Samuel Wharton?"

"Samuel?" Ms. Walcott asked. "I don't know. As far as I know, there was no Samuel in the Wharton family. And Jonas never spoke of a Samuel."

Maggie considered mentioning the portrait of Samuel Wharton she had seen in the secret passageway, but thought better of it. The last thing she needed now was to try and open the passageway only to have the knob not turn yet again.

"Jonas did come to be known as Old Man Wharton," Ms. Walcott continued. "He died about a year ago at age one hundred and two. I don't think he ever believed he would actually die. While he was alive, Mr. Wharton became more and more reclusive, and by the end of his life I was the only person who ever saw him. And while I worked here, I barely ever went into town."

"Interesting," Mr. Kim said. "Nice to know some of the history of this house."

"There is one more thing," Ms. Walcott continued. "Mr. Wharton's final wish was that his house never get turned into a ski lodge, and that no one ever go skiing here under any circumstances. I know he wrote it into his will, but his cousins must be ignoring it."

"Fat chance of that," Simon mumbled under his breath.

"Do you know why, Ms. Walcott?" Mrs. Kim asked.

"I don't know many of the details. I asked Jonas why once, and he got very angry. He refused to answer me and disappeared for a few days. What I do know is that there was some deeply tragic incident that led to Jonas closing down the slopes and vowing that no one would ever ski here again."

"This is the first time we're hearing about such a request," Mr. Kim explained. "Our understanding from the realtor is that the family is eager to sell, and they don't really care what becomes of the place."

"No, no! Ms. Walcott is right!" Maggie cried. "I told you we shouldn't buy this house. Old Man Wharton said so."

"Zip it, Maggie," Mrs. Kim warned.

"I'm just trying to stop us from making a horrible mistake!"

"Your daughter speaks wisely," Ms. Walcott said. "It would be best to honor Mr. Wharton's final wish."

"Yeah? And what's he gonna do if we don't?" Simon asked. "Come back from the dead and get us, like some ski-hating zombie?"

"Simon, don't be rude," Mrs. Kim snapped.

"Do not underestimate Jonas," Ms. Walcott said.

"He was a very powerful and determined man."

"Not anymore," Simon muttered under his breath, but loudly enough for everyone to hear.

"If any dead person can stop the living, I am certain that it is Jonas Wharton."

"That's who I saw!" Maggie exclaimed. "The night we arrived. In the window. It must have been Jonas Wharton watching us arrive."

"Maggie, that's enough!" Mr. Kim shouted. "We love this place. The house is perfect, the grounds are beautiful, and the mountain is ideal for skiing. No disrespect intended to you, Ms. Walcott, or to the memory of Mr. Wharton, but tomorrow my wife and I are going to talk to the bank about getting a loan to buy the place."

Mr. Kim continued, "The old Wharton Mansion will become the new Piney Hill Ski Resort."

A loud boom rocked the house, shaking the chandelier above the dining room table. Maggie felt her balance shift. She almost fell.

Then every light in the house went out!

# CHAPTER 6

"Where are those candles?" Mr. Kim shouted.

"Right here in this bag," his wife replied. "Just a moment."

Mrs. Kim fished a handful of candles out of a bag of emergency supplies she had packed, not knowing exactly what they would find when they arrived at the mansion. Once the candles were lit, Maggie looked around.

"Hey, where did Ms. Walcott go?" she asked.

"Maybe she had a date with Old Man Wharton's ghost," Simon quipped.

"Ms. Walcott? Are you all right?" Mrs. Kim called, but received no reply.

"I think turning out the lights is a bad joke, or a cheap scare tactic to try and frighten us so we don't buy this house," Mr. Kim said, the annoyance clear in his voice. "I'm sorry, Ms. Walcott, if you can hear me, but it's not going to work."

At that moment, everyone heard the front door slam shut.

Maggie raced to the front door. She wanted to talk with Ms. Walcott, to find out about Jonas Wharton, to confirm what she now believed—that Old Man Wharton's ghost was haunting this house.

Reaching the door, Maggie flung it open, only to see Ms. Walcott's footprints in the snow leading away from the door. The snow was coming down so heavily, the footprints were already being filled in. She heard a car door slam, then watched as Ms. Walcott sped down the driveway and away from the house.

"She's gone," Maggie reported.

"She left her things," Mrs. Kim said to no one in particular.

"Did anyone else think she was a bit odd?" Mr. Kim asked.

"Totally weird," Simon said.

"You're only saying that because she told you she didn't want you to go skiing," Maggie said.

"No, I'm saying that because she was talking about a dead guy haunting this house and trying to scare us away."

"Well, it would explain a lot," Maggie said, convinced now that they were dealing with a ghost. "The old man's face in the window, the lit candle that suddenly disappeared, the—"

"Are you still going on about that?" Mr. Kim said.

"Something is definitely going on here," Maggie defended herself. "And then there was the secret passageway."

"Wait, what?" her father asked.

Maggie forgot that she hadn't yet told them about that. "Last night, when everyone was asleep, I went back to the library. I found a secret passageway. It led to a strange room with all these pictures."

"What were you doing wandering around the house in the middle of the night anyway?" asked Simon.

"I had a bad dream," Maggie admitted. "I couldn't sleep."

"What kind of bad dream, honey?" Mrs. Kim asked.

"I dreamed I heard a voice and got out of bed to see who it was," Maggie began. "I saw the same old man I saw in the window—"

"Imagined you saw," Simon interrupted.

Maggie continued, "I followed him outside. He disappeared, and I got locked out during a big snowstorm. I woke up and went to explore."

"And it never occurred to you that you might have still been dreaming?" Simon asked.

"Just stop, Simon!" Maggie shouted. "You don't know what you're talking about. I believe that there is a ghost in this house. I do! You may think I'm crazy, but that's what I think. Besides, all you care about is your stupid skiing! Nothing else—"

"Maggie!" Mrs. Kim interrupted.

"Simon does have a good point, Mags," Mr. Kim said quietly. "Since you dreamed about seeing Old Man Wharton and getting locked out and all that, isn't it possible that you dreamed all this other stuff too?"

"No!" Maggie yelled. "I was not dreaming, or imagining, or whatever excuse you want to make. I know what I've been seeing. I've been seeing the ghost of Jonas Wharton. He never left this house, even after he died."

"Lower your voice, young lady," Mrs. Kim said. "We are going to the bank tomorrow. And if we get the loan, we are buying this place. And we will all live here. End of discussion!"

"Fine!" Maggie shouted back. "Then I'm going to bed!"

She got up and stormed away from the table, heading to her room.

"I'll go see if I can calm her down," Sophie said, excusing herself.

"Good luck with that," Simon mumbled.

"Thank you, Sophie," said Mrs. Kim.

A short while later, Maggie and Sophie were in their beds. A heavy silence hung in the room. Every so often Maggie let out a sigh of exasperation. Sophie bided her time, waiting for the right moment, hoping she could find just the thing to say to help her friend.

"It's a drag when no one believes you, Mags," Sophie said, finally breaking the silence. "I know. I've been there."

"Do *you* believe me?" Maggie asked softly.

"I don't know what to believe," Sophie admitted.

"Do you really think I can't tell the difference between having a dream and being awake?"

"Sometimes it's hard."

"Sophie, I know what I saw. My parents think I'm making this up because I don't want to live here."

"Well, you *don't* want to live here, right?"

"Yes, but why would I make up some crazy ghost story that no one would believe—"

"That no one *does* believe," Sophie corrected her friend.

"'That no one does believe?' Do you think I'm that lame?"

"No, of course not," said Sophie. "Let's do some more investigating tomorrow, okay?"

Having tried her best to help her friend, Sophie dozed off. Maggie, on the other hand, was wide awake, staring up at the pattern on the canopy. She had just about convinced herself that she was doomed to spend the rest of her life in this snowy wilderness, and nothing she could say or do would stop that from happening, when she heard something. Something strange, yet vaguely familiar.

A barely audible whisper. A raspy male voice.

*No, no, not again!* she thought.

The weak voice grew slightly louder.

Maggie started chanting in her head. *It's just the wind . . . it's just the wind . . . it's just the—*

"Leave this place!" the raspy voice said, still weakly,

but now loud enough for Maggie to make out the words.

"Leave this place!"

This time Maggie felt warm breath on her ear. She turned quickly, expecting to see someone, but no one was there.

*That is* not *the wind!*

Maggie threw her covers off and sat on the edge of her bed. She glanced over and saw Sophie peacefully snoring away. *I am* not *going on another wild ghost chase through this creepy old house only to have no one believe what I saw or heard.*

The voice came again, only this time it sounded as if it were coming from just outside the bedroom window.

Maggie stood up and threw on her slippers. She already regretted getting up as she walked toward the window.

Peering out, she saw only blowing, drifting snow.

"Leave this place," Maggie heard again. It sounded simultaneously like a whisper and like someone calling up to her from the ground below the window.

*I can't go out there alone,* Maggie thought. *Besides, I need Sophie to back up my story.*

"Sophie, wake up," she said softly.

Sophie didn't move.

"Sophie!" Maggie called a little louder.

Still nothing.

"Soph!" she cried, shaking the bed.

"Uhhhhh," Sophie moaned, rolling over. "What?"

"I hear a voice outside. I think it's Old Man Wharton. I'm going out to look, but I need you to come with me."

Sophie pulled the covers up over her head. "You're crazy if you're going out late at night in the freezing cold and snow. Have fun, but leave me alone. I'm asleep, see?"

She proceeded to fake an extremely loud snore.

"Leave this place!" the voice sounded from outside once again.

Maggie hurried back to the window. This time when she peered down, she saw letters being scratched in the snow. An *L*, then an *E*. There was no writer that Maggie could see.

"No!" she cried, realizing what the ghost was trying to spell.

This time she was not going to take no for an answer.

"Soph!" she yelled, pulling the covers off Sophie, grabbing her hand, and dragging her from her bed.

"You're crazy, Mags," Sophie moaned, stumbling to

the window. "And I am not going to—"

Sophie stopped in midsentence. Her jaw fell open, and she pointed down at the snow. Together, Maggie and Sophie watched the last letter being written. Another E.

"I see it, Mags! I see it!" she cried. "'Leave this place.' That's what it says. 'Leave this place.'"

"Nice to know I'm not completely crazy," Maggie replied. "Come on. We have to show the others. This proves that Old Man Wharton's ghost is haunting the house."

"Wait a minute, Mags," Sophie said, rubbing the sleep from her eyes. "Your parents might not believe that a ghost wrote it. They didn't see the letters being written as if no one was there. What if they think that Karina Walcott came back? She was very upset that your parents want to turn this house into a ski lodge."

"That's why I had to have you as a witness," Maggie said. "Now, come on. Let's get a closer look."

Snatching up her flashlight, Maggie tiptoed downstairs, followed closely by Sophie.

"Leave this place!" the voice said again, now clearly coming from right outside the front door.

Reaching the door, Maggie gripped the knob, took

a deep breath, threw it open, and stepped out into the swirling snow. *Please still be there,* she thought, having finally found an ally in Sophie, who stepped outside beside her.

She could barely see anything through the moving wall of white snow. Maggie's flashlight beam reflected right back against the snow, making it even harder to see.

"Where are you, Jonas?" she called out. "Why do you want us to leave?"

"Leave this place!" the voice repeated, sounding like it was coming from someone standing right next to her. But as best as Maggie could make out, she and Sophie were alone, standing in the freezing cold and raging snow.

# CHAPTER 7

"Where *are* you?" Maggie shouted through the blinding snow. "Show yourself! Stop torturing me!"

The fierce howling of the wind was the only reply she received.

"We've got to show the others," Maggie muttered. She turned around and ran through the open the front door and pounded up the stairs, tracking snow as she ran.

She burst into the room her parents were sleeping in and flipped on the light. "Mom! Dad! Get up!" she screamed, panic evident in her strained voice.

"What is it?" her dad asked, throwing the covers onto the floor and scrambling clumsily out of bed. "Is the house on fire? Did you get hurt? Is Simon okay?"

70

"Just come!" she yelled. "Both of you. You've got to come with me."

"All right, let me throw on my robe," Mr. Kim said, sliding his feet into his slippers.

"There had better be a good reason for waking us up in the middle of the night, young lady," Mrs. Kim said, rubbing her eyes and glancing at the clock. "I was sound asleep."

Maggie ran back out into the hall, then into Simon's room.

"Simon, get up!" she shouted.

"Whaaaa—" Simon mumbled.

"Get up!" Maggie yelled again, this time yanking the covers off her brother.

"Hey!" Simon shouted, sitting up and rubbing his face. "What's wrong with you? Have you gone insane? What do you want? I'm trying to sleep!"

"Get dressed and come downstairs. Mom and Dad are already up."

"Great time for a family picnic, Mags," Simon groaned, searching the floor for his robe.

Bounding back down the stairs, Maggie was soon joined by the others. Simon had put on his snow boots, still untied. His striped bathrobe peeked out from under his winter coat, which he had buttoned incorrectly. Adding to the comic picture was a floppy-eared hat resting on his mop of unkempt hair.

Sophie had now slipped her long down coat over her pajamas, but she still wore her slippers, having been unable to find her boots.

Mr. and Mrs. Kim looked like stuffed dolls. Each wore pajamas, a bathrobe, a sweater, and a winter coat, all in various stages of zipped, incorrectly buttoned, or not buttoned at all. Mr. Kim had decided to use the terry-cloth belt from his bathrobe to secure his winter coat. They both wore big snow boots on their feet.

Maggie grabbed the knob on the front door. "Okay, here it is. Proof that I'm not crazy. I'm not selfish. I'm not just making all this up because I don't want to live here. Ready?"

"To go out into the wind and snow at two thirty in the morning?" Mrs. Kim asked. "I don't imagine I'll ever be ready for that."

Maggie flung the front door open, and the whole crew stepped outside.

They were immediately assaulted by wind-driven

snow, which stung the inadequately protected areas of their exposed skin.

"There!" Maggie shouted triumphantly, pointing at the spot where she had seen the message scrawled into the snow. "Now do you believe me? Now that you see it for yourself?"

"See *what*?" Mr. Kim asked. "What are we supposed to be seeing?"

Glancing down at the snowy ground, Maggie realized that the message she had seen scratched into the snow had vanished—covered over or blown away by the wind and drifting snow.

"NO! It was just here. A message from him. From Old Man Wharton, telling us to leave." Maggie swept the flashlight across the snow-covered ground, desperately searching for the message, but it was gone—completely vanished. The wind—or someone—had wiped it out, replacing it with new snow.

"Sophie saw it too!" Maggie cried.

"Is this true, Sophie?"

"Yes, Mrs. Kim," Sophie replied as stunned as Maggie that the writing that had been there moments earlier was now gone without a trace. "We saw it being written, but there was no writer that we could see."

"Well, then you're both crazy," Simon said. "Way to go, Mags. Wake everyone up because you had a bad dream. I'm going back to bed. I hope Old Man Wharton hasn't stolen my blanket."

He hurried back into the house, followed by the others.

"I've tried to be tolerant, Maggie, I really have," Mrs. Kim said, once inside. She shook the snow off her coat, hair, and boots. "But I am so very disappointed in this blatantly selfish behavior. We all know you don't want to move here, but to wake everyone up for nothing? This has gone too far. It's time you think of someone else in this family besides just yourself."

"But Sophie saw—"

Mrs. Kim hurried up the stairs without saying another word.

"This was a real bonehead stunt, Maggie," her dad said. "I don't even know what to say, so I'll go upstairs too. Good night."

Maggie flopped down into a chair, feeling defeated.

"I saw it, Mags," Sophie said. "I believe you. And I'm starting to think I believe in Old Man Wharton's ghost, too."

"Thanks, Soph," Maggie said softly. "I'll tell you what I believe. I believe I'm going to be living here."

"I'll visit," Sophie promised.

Maggie smiled, then the two girls trudged up the stairs. They slipped into the room and back into bed. Tossing and turning, Maggie tried to push everything that had happened out of her mind. Eventually she fell asleep.

She was startled awake by a voice shouting at her.

"Leave this place!"

"Leave this place!" she heard the voice repeat, shouting so loudly Maggie was certain that whoever it was had to be right there in the room. And also certain that now, finally, everyone else had heard it as well.

She leaped from her bed and looked around. There was no one else in the room, not even Sophie. Sophie's bed looked as if it had not even been slept in.

Maggie ran from the room, stopping short at the top of the stairs. There, scrawled in dripping red paint—or was it blood?—in huge letters painted on the wall were the same three words that had been plaguing her since her arrival: LEAVE THIS PLACE!

She bounded down the stairs and stumbled into

the dining room. There she saw the same three words crudely carved into the dining room table: LEAVE THIS PLACE!

Maggie staggered backward and bumped into someone. Spinning around, she found herself face-to-face with Old Man Wharton. His empty black eye sockets peered down at her. Through rotted teeth and foul-smelling breath he barked, "LEAVE THIS PLACE!"

"No! No! No!" Maggie screamed over and over.

"Maggie, wake up! Wake up!"

Maggie opened her eyes and stared up at Sophie, who had been shaking her for almost a full minute.

"You were shouting in your sleep," Sophie said as Maggie sat up.

Maggie breathed deeply, glad that it was just a dream. But she started to wonder if everything that had happened last night was a dream. Had she dreamed that Sophie also saw the writing in the snow? Was she still the only one who believed in the ghost of Old Man Wharton?

"Uh, Soph, did you see something weird tonight?" Maggie asked tentatively.

"You mean, you screaming 'No! No! No!' in your

sleep?" Sophie replied. "Unless, of course, you mean the writing in the snow?"

"Oh, Sophie, you have no idea how relieved I am." Maggie sighed and hugged her friend.

"Well, don't be so relieved yet," Sophie said. "We still have to convince the rest of your family that this house is haunted!"

# CHAPTER 8

"Pass the orange juice, Soph," Maggie said sleepily across the breakfast table later that morning. She had gotten very little sleep the previous night, and she now sat with her elbows on the table and her chin resting in her hands. Even pouring orange juice into a glass seemed to take major effort.

"You look wiped, Mags," Sophie commented, having not gotten all that much sleep herself.

Maggie groaned, rubbing her eyes with her palms.

"Eggs, anyone?" Mr. Kim asked cheerfully, leaning over Sophie's plate with a panful of scrambled eggs in his hand.

"Thanks, Mr. Kim," Sophie said.

"You still mad at me, Dad?" asked Maggie, waving away a large spoonful of eggs.

"Nah!" Mr. Kim exclaimed, smiling. "Nothing could get me down today. Today your mother and I are going to the bank to finalize the loan so we can buy this place and transform it from the old Wharton Mansion into . . . drumroll, please . . . the Piney Hill Ski Resort!

"That is, if your mother finishes getting ready anytime soon," he added, glancing at his watch.

"What was that, dear?" said Mrs. Kim, strolling into the dining room.

"I said, I can't wait to see how lovely you'll look once you're all ready for our big day," Mr. Kim lied.

"Uh-huh," Mrs. Kim replied. "Good try. Sad, but a good try."

At that moment Simon came bounding down the stairs.

"Good morning, family!" he announced energetically. "And what a beautiful morning it is!"

"What do you want, Simon?" Maggie asked. "You're never this nice unless you want something."

"Maggie, what a terrible thing to say about your brother," Mrs. Kim said.

"Just wait," said Maggie. "I'm not wrong."

The Kims didn't have to wait long.

"So Mom, I was thinking that since it has stopped

snowing and it's a beautiful, sunny day, maybe I could check out the skiing at the future Piney Hill Ski Resort!" Simon asked.

"What a terrible thing I said, huh, Mom?" said Maggie, smiling for the first time that morning.

"That's enough, Maggie," Mrs. Kim replied, then she turned to Simon. "I don't want you to go skiing when your father and I aren't here. We'll be at the bank and won't be around if anything goes wrong."

Simon's entire demeanor changed instantly. His mood shifted from happy-go-lucky to huffy faster than Maggie could say, I told you so.

"But Mom," he whined, "nothing is gonna go wrong. I'm practically a pro skier. Coach MacLean said he thought that if I practiced just a little more, I'd be good enough to try out for the Olympic team next year. So I should definitely practice today."

"I know how good you are, dear," Mrs. Kim said sympathetically. "But I'm just not comfortable knowing that you'd be way up on the mountain when we're not around."

"We promise you can go tomorrow when we'll be here," Mr. Kim added.

"In the meantime, however, it is strictly forbidden

for any of you to go skiing when we are not home," Mrs. Kim stated sternly. "Is that clear?"

Simon just shook his head, got up from the table, and trudged back upstairs.

*So it's gonna be just me, Sophie, and Simon here by ourselves to deal with Old Man Wharton's ghost today,* Maggie thought.

"Okay, have fun, everyone," Mrs. Kim said, gathering up some papers she would need at the bank. "We might grab some lunch in town and check out a few stores, so we probably won't be back till after dark."

"And hopefully we'll be back with good news!" Mr. Kim announced as he and his wife headed out the front door.

"Bye!" Mrs. Kim waved.

Barely a minute had passed after Mr. and Mrs. Kim's car pulled out of the driveway when Simon came tearing down the stairs. This time he was dressed in his full ski outfit.

"Hey, where are you going?" Maggie asked.

"What's it look like?" Simon retorted. "I'm hitting the slopes, Mags."

"But what about Mom and Dad?"

"As they so eloquently pointed out over and over, they're not home."

"But what if they find out?"

"Who's gonna tell them? You?"

"No, but—"

"Catch you later, Mags." Simon snatched up his skis and headed for the door.

"Be careful, you big lunk," Maggie insisted, trailing behind him.

"Relax," Simon cooed. "I'm in great shape. I can handle these slopes. And I'll be back before sunset. I promise. Piece of cake. What can go wrong?"

Maggie and Sophie followed Simon outside. He was right. It was a bright, clear, sunny day. The previous day's snowfall sparkled in the cold, still air.

"Be careful!" Maggie shouted after her brother, just before he disappeared into a grove of glistening pine trees at the base of the tall mountain that would become the main ski slope if all went well at the bank.

Maggie's stomach began to drop. She felt a bit nauseous.

"I've got a bad feeling about this, Sophie," she said, turning back toward the house. "A really bad feeling."

# CHAPTER 9

Maggie and Sophie stepped back inside. Settling into the living room, they wondered what they would do all day. They definitely didn't want another ghostly encounter. Maggie pulled out her cell phone.

"Ugh, just habit," she groaned. "No cell phone service here. I forgot for a moment!"

She turned off her phone and booted up her laptop. "Maybe I can glom on to someone's wi-fi."

"Really, like whose wi-fi?" said Sophie. "A bear's? A raccoon's?"

"Yeah," Maggie muttered, slamming down the lid of her computer. "Nothing. No cell service, no Internet. What are people supposed to do here? It's like living in the Stone Age."

"I don't know what you're going to do after you move here," Sophie said.

"Don't even say those words, Soph. Maybe someone robbed the bank and they don't have any money left to loan to my parents."

"But for today, there's still lots of house to explore," Sophie offered.

Maggie's expression changed instantly.

Now that she firmly believed that the house really was being haunted by the ghost of Old Man Wharton, her desire to poke into dark corners had lessened considerably.

"I don't know, Soph," she said. "After what we saw last night, I'm pretty afraid of this place."

"Good point," Sophie said. "Although it definitely seems less creepy here during the day."

"All right," Maggie agreed. "But don't walk too far away from me."

Maggie and Sophie roamed from room to room without finding much of interest at first. Most of the rooms were empty of furniture, filled only with cobwebs and dust.

Then they stepped into what had obviously once

been a grand ballroom. A huge chandelier dangled from the center of the ceiling.

"Wow, Mags, look at this room," said Sophie, spinning around and lifting her hands to grab the hem of an imaginary ball gown. For a moment, she forgot about Old Man Wharton and her apprehension about being alone in this haunted old mansion. She was swept away by the thought of going to a dance in a ballroom like this one.

Sophie began to waltz around the room. "Can't you just picture fancy parties for beautiful people, with a string quartet playing?"

Maggie joined her, and the two girls danced around the wide-plank wooden floor, spinning and giggling as they went, as imaginary music played beautifully in their heads.

The two friends were suddenly shaken from their fantasy by a crashing sound coming from another room.

"What was that?" Maggie cried, clutching Sophie's arm.

"We are definitely not alone in this house!" Sophie replied, walking slowly to the ballroom door.

She peeked around back out into the hall. She saw no one.

"Where did that crash come from?" Maggie asked.

"Let's go find out," Sophie said, stepping from the ballroom.

"Wait," Maggie said, grabbing Sophie's arm. "I'm really scared."

"But aren't you curious?" Sophie asked. "Not just about what caused that crash, but about the whole ghost thing?"

"I don't know, Soph," Maggie replied. "All I wanted was to prove to my parents that this place is haunted so they wouldn't buy it. But now that we're alone in the house, I'm terrified. I mean, what if the ghost wants to hurt us? There's no one here to help. It could be hours before Simon or my parents come back. What if something really bad happens? What if—"

"Whoa, slow down. You're working yourself into a frenzy here. Based on everything he's done so far, Old Man Wharton seems more intent on scaring us away than on actually hurting anyone."

"I just have this terrible feeling that something awful is going to happen today," Maggie explained. "I can't shake it."

"Let's go see if we can put that feeling to rest," Sophie said, taking her friend by the hand and leading her into the hallway.

One by one, the girls opened each door they came to. The first room looked like an art gallery. Huge framed paintings lined the walls. Most of the art depicted beautiful landscapes shown during various seasons.

"These might be worth something," Sophie said. "And they just left them here."

"Maybe the cousins who were fighting over the place don't know they're here," Sophie said. "That Walcott lady said that no one has been in the house since Wharton died."

The next room contained a grand piano, many music stands still holding sheet music, and a violin, which rested in a corner. Fancy wooden folding chairs were set up as if for a concert.

"Back in the old days, people invited their friends over and played music, just for fun," Sophie said.

"Life without iPods, huh," Maggie added, trying to keep her mood up, despite her feelings of dread. They stepped from the room and closed the door.

The two friends continued down the hall. Maggie felt grim again almost instantly.

"We still haven't found whatever it was that made that crashing noise," she pointed out to Sophie.

"Uh, I think we just did," Sophie replied, opening

the next door along the hallway and peeking in.

Stepping into the room, they discovered framed photographs hung on the wall and placed on shelves. Sophie pointed to a rectangular shape on the wall, at the top of which hung an empty picture hook. Glancing down, she spotted a framed photo lying on the floor, surrounded by shattered glass.

"There," she said. "Where that photograph had obviously been hanging for a long time. That's what fell and crashed."

Maggie hurried over and picked up the photo from the floor. She carefully turned it over. Additional shards of what had been the protective glass tumbled down and shattered.

Maggie and Sophie stared at the black-and-white photograph of two men standing outside in a winter wonderland. The men bore some resemblance to each other. They each had an arm around the other's shoulder. One was much older than the other.

The older one was dressed in a thick sweater and a cap that nearly coverd his eyes. The other was wearing a ski outfit complete with gloves and goggles and clutched a pair of skis, which stood upright in his hand.

It was hard to tell who either was with their caps and goggles on, but Maggie couldn't help but wonder if she'd seen these faces before. She also didn't feel much like thinking about it, not after everything that had been happening.

"Old Man Wharton's ghost must have knocked this off the wall!" Maggie concluded. "And I don't think it's coincidence that of all the pictures in this room, he chose the one that had a skier in it. He's trying to send us a message. Just like Ms. Walcott said. He's upset that my parents are going to turn his home into a ski resort!"

Sophie shivered. "He's not some random spirit that people catch a glimpse of, or a ghost who makes the temperature in a room drop suddenly. Old Man Wharton is walking around knocking pictures off the wall. And specific pictures about a specific subject, too."

"I don't need to explore anymore, Soph," Maggie said anxiously. "I think we should just hang out until my parents get back. Then of course we've got to find a way to prove to them that the ghost is real. If we show them this smashed photo, they'll just think I did it."

The two friends headed back to the kitchen for a little lunch, then hunkered down in the living room, spending the rest of the afternoon munching on snacks, flipping through magazines, and chatting about school—the one they both currently attended back in the suburbs.

As the afternoon wore on and the light grew dimmer, Maggie thought about her brother.

"Hey, Simon told us he'd be back before sunset," she said, peering out the window. "The sun's going to drop behind that mountain in a few minutes, so where is he?"

Sophie put down her magazine and joined her friend at the window. The last reddish-orange rays of sunshine spilled out onto the pristine whiteness, sending off a lustrous glow.

"I don't like this, Soph," Maggie said after a few seconds. "I didn't like it when he left this morning, and I really don't like it now."

"Let's give him a few more minutes," Sophie said, trying to sound as reassuring as she could. "He probably just wanted to go on one more run. You know Simon and his skiing."

"I don't know," Maggie grumbled. "I have a—"

"I know, a bad feeling about this. Just sit down for a few minutes. Staring out the window isn't going to make him appear."

Maggie fell into a chair and picked up the magazine

she had been reading. About ten seconds passed before she dropped the magazine onto the table, got up, and looked out the window again.

Still no sign of Simon.

Returning to her chair, Maggie had barely sat down and picked up the magazine when she popped back up. This time when she looked out the window, she saw that the snow had taken on a blue tinge as the last rays of sunlight vanished behind the mountain.

"Something's wrong," she said. "I know it."

"What should we do?" Sophie asked.

"I don't know. My parents are due back any moment, and if Simon isn't here when they get home, he's going to be in big trouble. We have to go find him, Soph."

Maggie slid on her snow boots and slipped into her down jacket.

"Well, I'm not going to let you go out there alone," Sophie said as she began to bundle herself up.

Maggie grabbed two flashlights and threw them into a backpack. The two stepped out into the cold indigo twilight and trudged off in the direction they had seen Simon go earlier. They soon reached the base of the mountain and began the arduous climb to the top.

Snow crept in over the tops of Maggie's boots, and she felt her toes get cold and wet. The climb grew more difficult with each step. The air got colder and the light faded.

"Simon!" Maggie shouted in a strained voice. Her breath was visible in the frosty air.

"Simon!" Sophie joined in, yelling at the top of her lungs.

The only answer they received was the hollow echo of their own voices bouncing off the mountain.

"Simon!" Maggie shouted again. This time she got an answer, but not the one she was hoping for.

A-OOOOOOOO! came a fierce howling that sliced through the still, late-afternoon air.

"What is that? What is that?" Maggie cried, panic flooding her entire being.

"Coyotes," Sophie replied in a surprisingly calm voice.

"Coyotes!" Maggie screamed. "What are they doing here?"

"They *live* here."

"How do you know what a coyote sounds like? You've lived in the suburbs your whole life, just like me."

"My uncle has a cabin in the woods a couple hours north of here, remember?" Sophie explained.

"Oh yeah. I forgot about that," Maggie replied.

*A-OOOOOOOO!* The howling came again, louder this time.

"And we spent a week up there last summer. The main entertainment was sitting on the front porch at night, listening to the coyotes howl," Sophie said.

*A-OOOOOOOO!*

"Simon! Where are you?" Maggie shrieked, doing her best to continue forcing one foot in front of the other as she made her way up the mountain.

The light was almost gone. Maggie and Sophie were having trouble seeing where they were going.

"Turn on the flashlights," Maggie said.

Snow started falling.

"Great," Sophie groaned as her light blazed on. Thick snowflakes shimmered in the beam, picking up in intensity with each strenuous step they took.

"It's really dark," Sophie said, whipping her flashlight back and forth. It sliced through the falling snow, illuminating only the fact that being able to see was growing more difficult by the second.

"Are we lost?" Sophie asked, sounding scared for the first time. "What if we get lost in the dark and freeze to death in the snow? What if we fall and break our legs and the coyotes come and—"

"Soph! Stop! Look. We're just about at the top of the mountain. Come on!"

Tapping into some unknown reserve of energy, Maggie picked up her pace, pushing on. A few minutes later, she paused near the top of the mountain.

"Almost there, Soph!" she cried.

Turning back she saw no sign of Sophie.

"Sophie! Where are you?" she called out, her flashlight not much help in the driving snow.

"Right here," Sophie wheezed, staggering through the snow until she reached Maggie. "You moved too fast. I'm wiped out. Now what?"

"I don't know," Maggie said, squinting to see better, trying to get her bearings.

"Are we even going to find our way back to the house?" Sophie asked, her voice trembling as much from fear as from the cold. "Are we going to—"

"There!" Maggie cried, pointing her flashlight down at the ground. "Footprints!"

"Simon!" Sophie yelled.

Leading the way, with Sophie straggling along

behind her, Maggie tried to follow the footprints. They led right to the top of the mountain.

"He was here!" Maggie cried. "Simon! Where are you?"

"Look, Mags!" Sophie shouted, pointing just ahead. "The footprints change to ski tracks right there. He must have climbed up to this point, then skied down the other side of the mountain."

Maggie forced herself to move even faster. Now Sophie was right at her side. Together they rounded the top of the mountain and began to follow the ski tracks down.

The fresh coating of snow made it harder to follow the tracks. It also hid the fact that the slope of the mountain dropped off sharply and suddenly.

Both girls lost their footing at the same moment and started tumbling down the mountain.

"Ahhh!" they both screamed, but their cries of terror were muffled by the pummeling they were receiving as they rolled down the mountain, completely out of control.

"I can't stop!" Maggie cried, growing dizzy as she spun head over heels again and again, bouncing, skidding, and sliding downhill faster than she'd thought she could go.

Maggie finally reached the bottom and rolled to a stop. Sophie crashed into her and the two were still for a moment, catching their breath as the snow fell down on them.

"You okay?" Sophie finally asked.

"I think so," Maggie replied, struggling to stand up.

"My flashlight!" Sophie cried. "It's gone! I must have lost it as I fell."

Maggie looked down. Somehow, her flashlight was still in her hand. She flicked the switch a few times, but it remained dark. The sun was now completely gone. Pitch-black darkness had enveloped them like a thick, impenetrable blanket.

"Come on, come on, come on!" Maggie yelled at the flashlight. She whacked it with the heel of her hand, and the light popped on.

Sweeping the light along the ground, Maggie gasped in horror. There in the narrow pool of light lay Simon's broken skis. Simon himself was nowhere to be seen.

# CHAPTER 10

"Simon!" Maggie screamed, her throat aching from all the shouting, the cold, and the overwhelming exhaustion that had begun to overtake her. "Where is he? These are his skis, but they're all busted up. Simon!"

"There must have been an accident," Sophie said, peering through the darkness, then feeling foolish for thinking she might be able to see anything.

"Okay, but where is he?" Maggie asked. "Why would he just leave his skis?"

"Maybe he tried to walk back to the house," Sophie suggested. "He could be anywhere."

Maggie aimed her flashlight back up the mountain, hoping to see footprints leading up and toward the house. She saw none. Turning back around, she spotted something.

"Look!" Maggie called out. Her flashlight lit up a clearly visible set of footprints leading not back up the mountain, but farther away on this side, into a grove of tall pines. "That way. He went that way."

Being extremely careful not to obliterate the footprints, Maggie and Sophie hurried along beside them, following the prints into the wooded area.

In the pine grove the footprints were even more visible, as the thick trees caught much of the newly fallen snow in their branches, and less snow reached the ground.

"My parents are totally gonna freak out when they get home and find all three of us gone," Maggie said, her mind jumping to the second most pressing situation at hand.

"Let's just find Simon and deal with one thing at a time," Sophie said, trying to help her friend calm down.

"And what if Simon is really hurt? Or worse?" Maggie said. "This is all so bad, so very, very bad. If we find him, and he's all right, I'm gonna kill him for making us come out here and worry so much!"

Rounding a bend, the footprints turned onto a narrow path between trees. As they walked single file now, with Maggie in the lead lighting the way, the night seemed to grow darker and more threatening with each step they took. Then she spotted something in the distance.

"Look, Soph, it's some kind of building! Hurry!"

The snow was piled high in the narrow path between the trees. Stepping over fallen branches, sinking into mounds of drifted snow, the girls approached the small structure.

"It's a shed," Maggie said as her flashlight reflected in a window. "Out here in the middle of the woods. What's it doing here?"

Tromping the last few yards, the girls reached the structure. They peered into the window to discover stacks of books scattered everywhere. Maggie spied an old wooden desk buried under mounds of paper. Worn-out chairs and ancient reading lamps filled the cramped, obviously neglected room.

"It looks like an office or a study," Maggie said. "But one that hasn't been used in years."

"Maybe it was a secret getaway, or—" Sophie started.

"Simon!" Maggie suddenly shrieked. "It's Simon!"

Sophie stared into the shed and saw Maggie's

brother lying on the floor in the corner.

Kicking up snow in spraying curtains of white, Maggie ran around to the front door of the shed, only to discover that it was padlocked.

"Someone locked him inside!" Maggie cried, yanking on the thick metal lock.

"Maggie, he's not moving!" Sophie called, still peering through the window.

Desperately looking around, Maggie spotted an old pile of firewood covered in snow. She grabbed the biggest piece she could find and dragged it back to the door.

"Help me," she said, getting as good a grip as possible on the snow-covered chunk of wood.

Sophie wrapped her arm around the log to take some of the weight from Maggie. Together they lifted the wood above their heads.

"Ready? One, two, three!"

With all the strength they could muster, the girls slammed the log down onto the padlock. The wood hit the bottom of the lock, sending it spinning around, but not damaging it in any way. The log flew from their hands and landed with a dull thud in the snow.

"Again," Maggie cried, panting from the effort.

"This time we have to hit the top of the lock where it's thinnest."

Kneeling down in the snow, Maggie hoisted the log up with both hands. Sophie got a grip too, and once again they lifted the wood high into the air.

"One, two, three . . . GO!"

Aiming for the thin loop at the top of the lock, the girls hit their target and smashed the lock open. They let the log fall, then Maggie yanked off the broken lock and threw open the door.

Rushing inside, she dropped to the floor beside her brother.

"Simon," she whispered softly into his ear.

He didn't stir.

"Simon," she repeated, shaking him gently. "Please answer me."

"Urrrrgh," Simon groaned, rolling awkwardly onto his side.

Maggie helped him up into a sitting position. He blinked a few times, then rubbed his head and winced.

"What happened to you?" Maggie asked.

Simon moaned again.

"Give him a second, Mags," Sophie interjected.

"I don't know," Simon said in a weak, raspy voice. "I hadn't been outside for more than fifteen minutes, when I felt something push me. Maybe it was the wind, but it felt like someone knocked me down. I looked back right before I fell, and I think I saw a man standing there. But that was probably just my imagination. That's the last thing I remember. Next thing I know, you're waking me up here in this . . . this . . . where am I, anyway?'

"I have no idea what this is, but the important thing is that we found you," Maggie said, helping her brother to his feet.

"What time is it?" Simon said, looking around in a panic. "Mom and Dad? Are they home? Do they know I went skiing even when they said not to?"

"I don't know," Maggie replied. "They weren't home when we left, but . . ." She trailed off.

"So we'd better get home, like, now!" Sophie finished.

The three kids hurried from the shed. Just before she stepped outside, Maggie spotted an old scrapbook sitting on a small table. For some reason, she snatched it up and slipped it into her backpack.

Outside the shed, they were immediately assaulted by the wind and biting snow.

"We only have one flashlight," Maggie said. "Follow me."

She guided the others through the pine grove, out to the base of the mountain.

"Are you going to be able to climb?" Sophie asked Simon.

"Do I have any other choice? Unless you guys want to carry me."

The three began the long, arduous trudge up the mountain, guided only by Maggie's single flashlight beam. Simon stumbled into the snow a few times, and the girls helped him up, but he pushed himself forward.

Maggie thought about how close she had just come to losing her only brother.

"Can you remember anything else about what happened?" she asked as they reached the top of the mountain and paused. A soft glow poured from the windows of the house.

"I'm not sure," Simon said as the trio hurried down the steep slope. "If someone did push me, who could it have been?"

"Old Man Wharton," Maggie said without hesitation. "His ghost."

"Are you still going on about that?" Simon asked. "I don't know who the guy was."

Maggie fished in her pocket and pulled out her cell phone.

"Who ya gonna call, Mags?" Simon said, smiling for a moment at his little joke. "You know there's no cell service up here."

"I'm not calling anyone," she said, frantically scrolling through all the pictures she had stored on her camera.

"Was it *this* old guy, Simon?" Maggie asked, shoving the phone into Simon's face. "This is the picture I took of the face in the window. It's gotta be the ghost of Old Man Wharton."

He squinted at the glowing image, and his face turned pale.

"That's him!" he cried. "I couldn't make it out the first time you showed it to me, but now that I know what I'm looking for, I can see the face—his face, the face of the man who pushed me!"

Maggie felt an enormous sense of relief. Not only had she found her brother, but he now knew what she and Sophie knew: This house, this property, was haunted by the ghost of Old Man Wharton. She hugged Simon tightly.

"I don't mean to break up this little celebration, but what about your parents?" Sophie asked.

"Can you see if they're home?" Simon asked.

"I don't see any movement in the house," Sophie said, looking down the hill.

A few minutes later they reached the base of the mountain. At that moment they spotted headlights pulling into the driveway.

"Mom and Dad are home!" Maggie cried. "We are *so* busted!"

# CHAPTER 11

"Hurry!" Maggie urged. "We can make it! Come on!"

"No way!" Sophie cried. "We're gonna run into them at the front door!"

"That's why we're going through the *back* door!"

Running as quickly as they could through the snow, Maggie, Sophie, and Simon raced around to the back of the mansion. Bursting into the house through the back door, they threw off their snow-encrusted coats, hats, and gloves, and yanked off their heavy boots.

"They'll know we were out in the snow when they see this pile of stuff," Simon worried, hopping on one foot, struggling to pull his boot off.

"So, we went out for a snowball fight, that's all!" Maggie replied.

When their snowy jackets and boots had all been shed, they dashed into the living room.

Sophie lit several candles. Maggie tossed a magazine to Simon and picked another up for herself.

Footsteps sounded near the front door.

"Simon!" Maggie cried, pointing at her brother. "Your clothes!"

"What?" he asked, looking down at his signature ski outfit. "Oh." He bounded up the stairs just as the front door swung open.

"Hey, gang, we're home!" Mr. Kim announced.

"Sorry we're late," Mrs. Kim added as she and her husband took off their coats. "The roads are getting very slippery with all this snow. It took us over an hour to get back from town."

"Hope you guys weren't too bored, just sitting around here all day," Mr. Kim said.

"We're okay, Dad," Maggie said, offering no details and certainly no clues as to the adventure they had just survived.

"Where's Simon?" Mrs. Kim asked.

"Right here, Mom," Simon said, walking slowly down the stairs, wearing his pajamas. He rubbed his eyes.

Maggie and Sophie exchanged a look.

"I must have dozed off," Simon lied. "What time is it anyway?"

"Time for great news!" Mr. Kim exclaimed, unable to keep his excitement hidden any longer. "The bank approved our loan. It's official—we're going to buy this place!"

"It's all downhill from here," said Mrs. Kim, hoping her little joke would help get the kids excited about the news. "Smooth sailing. The hard part is done."

No one said a word. Even Simon stared down at his feet.

"Well, don't everyone get too excited," Mr. Kim said, shaking his head. "Is everything all right here? Did something happen today?"

Simon looked up. "What do you mean?" he asked nervously.

"Well, Simon, I thought you, at least, would be happy about this," Mr. Kim explained. "This means that once we fix up the slopes, you'll be able to ski anytime you want. I figured you'd be jumping for joy."

Simon looked over at Maggie and Sophie. Even though he still wasn't sure there was a ghost, he now believed that someone—or something—was trying to scare his family away. But he certainly couldn't tell his parents about the events that had led to his discovery.

"I don't know, Dad," he began, his mind racing to come up with some kind of excuse. "I guess now that it's real, I feel a little overwhelmed."

"Look, I know this is going to be a big change for you, for all of us," Mr. Kim said sympathetically. "But opportunities like this don't come around every day. Just give it a chance."

"What choice do I have?" Maggie asked, pointing out the obvious.

"I'll start dinner," Mrs. Kim said, heading for the kitchen.

"I'll help," Mr. Kim added, sighing deeply. "Let's leave the Gloomy Guses to themselves."

When they had left the room, Simon leaned in close to Maggie. "I have to tell you, Mags," he began, speaking softly so his parents couldn't hear. "When you started with all this ghost stuff and disappearing candles and writing in the snow, I thought you were just being a brat. But now I believe something is going on."

"The question is, what are we going to do about it?"

Maggie replied. "Even though we all now believe that there's a ghost here, Mom and Dad will never believe us."

"I'm scared to spend one more night here," Sophie said. "And the thought of you guys living here all the time . . ." Her words trailed off.

"I thought you were just being difficult before," Simon continued. "But after what just happened to me, I have to agree with you. I think that buying this house would be the worst idea ever."

"What *did* happen to you?" Sophie asked.

"I got up to the top of the hill just fine. As soon as I put on my skis, I felt a pair of hands shove me in the back. I wasn't ready at all. I was in no position to speed down such a steep hill. That takes preparation, proper form, and complete concentration. My point is that someone pushed me. As I sped away, I twisted around. I could make out the face of an old man, smiling."

"Old Man Wharton," Maggie said.

"It must be," Simon agreed. "When I got to the bottom of the hill, my skis must have been broken. I probably wandered into that shed, dazed from everything, and then he locked me in."

"What's to stop him from really hurting us?" Maggie

wondered aloud. She looked right at Simon. "By attacking you, he's shown us that he's capable of violent action, not just pranks. I'm with Sophie—I don't want to stay here another night."

Sophie added, "Especially since your parents just announced to everyone here—living or dead—that they're definitely buying the place. I'm on pins and needles that at any second the lights are going to go off again, or something will explode, or the house will catch on fire, or—"

"What are we going to do about it?" Maggie asked. She leaned onto her backpack and felt something hard inside. Opening the flap, she pulled out the scrapbook she had snatched from the shed.

Keeping one eye out for her parents, she slowly opened the dusty, battered cover.

Old photos filled the book. Maggie recognized images of various rooms in the house, but mostly they were pictures of people she didn't recognize.

"Look at this," she said. "Pages from a diary."

"What's it say? Whose diary?" Sophie asked, peering over Maggie's shoulder at the yellowed pages pasted into the scrapbook.

Maggie began reading. "'January 21, 1951. Watched

Samuel head off to the mountain, skis in hand, as usual. He seems to love skiing more now that he has become an adult.' The rest is torn off."

"There's that Samuel guy again!" said Sophie. "Ernest built the place, and Jonas is Old Man Wharton, the one who died and refuses to leave. But Samuel?"

"Jonas's brother!" Maggie said in an excited whisper that came out a bit louder than she had intended. "Look at this picture."

"Maggie, did you say something, dear?" Mrs. Kim called out from the kitchen.

"Nothing, Mom."

"Dinner will be ready in about half an hour," her mother continued.

"Here's a picture of Samuel Wharton," Maggie said. "Look familiar, Soph?"

"We saw a picture of this same guy in that storage room," Sophie recalled. "Remember, in that pile of old photographs we saw?"

"Exactly," said Maggie. "And the portrait I saw at the entrance to the secret room, and all the other ones inside. And I'll bet the photo that crashed to the floor was a picture of Jonas and Samuel."

"Um, did I miss something?" Simon asked. "What does this have to do with anything?"

"I don't know," Maggie replied, flipping through the pages of the diary. "Here's another entry." They leaned over to read it together.

March 28, 1955. Still a decent amount of snow on the mountain. Yet with the days growing longer and warmer as spring makes its approach, Samuel grows mournful, worrying that each day he sets out to ski might be his last for many months.

He always dreads our return to the city for the summer; he misses the mountain so. And although I am getting too old for skiing, I am beginning to see why Samuel loves it so much. More often, it seems, I contemplate remaining here year round.

This entry had a piece of a signature. It read *Jona*. The rest was smudged and torn.

"Jonas!" Maggie cried.

"What?" her dad called from the kitchen.

"Nothing, Dad, we're just playing a game," Maggie replied.

"Games are good!" came the response from the kitchen.

"So that confirms it. This is Old Man Wharton's scrapbook, complete with pages from his diary," Maggie continued.

"So that shed obviously was his private place!" Sophie commented, shaking her head. "He must have gone there to write in his diary."

Maggie kept flipping through the book. Pages and pages later she came to a brittle, yellowed newspaper clipping dated February 9, 1970, with a headline that read SAMUEL WHARTON DIES IN SKIING ACCIDENT.

"Whoa!" Simon said, leaning in close to get a better look.

Maggie read the article aloud. "'Thirty-eight-year-old Samuel Wharton, a local skiing enthusiast and member of the prestigious Wharton family, died yesterday in a tragic skiing accident on family property. Mr. Wharton, who never married, is survived by his older brother, Jonas Wharton.'"

Maggie and Sophie both turned to look at Simon. Maggie's mind flashed back to the fact that her brother had just gone skiing on the same mountain where Samuel Wharton had died.

"What?" he said defensively. "They had primitive equipment back then. Who knows what that Samuel dude was using. I—"

Maggie threw her arms around Simon and hugged him tightly. She thought about the old ski equipment that had been arranged as a shrine in the secret room—obviously done by Jonas Wharton in memory of his dead brother.

"Guys, look at this," Sophie said urgently, flipping the scrapbook to the next page. "It's Old Man Wharton's diary, dated February 12, 1970, a few days after Samuel died." They all peered over the book.

It is with a heart full of burning grief that I put pen to paper. I buried Samuel today. It took every ounce of self-control to not climb into the grave with him.

A part of me died today, as if I

had lost a limb or a vital organ from my own body. Samuel was my beloved younger brother. I practically raised him, and he was all I had. There are no more relatives, none that speak to me or deem me worthy of a visit, at any rate. And as for friends, well, I have scant use for them anymore.

I can scarcely breathe, as if all the oxygen in the world was buried beside dear Samuel. One thing is for certain. No one will ever ski on my mountain again. Not for any reason.

I fear these may be the last words I ever record, regardless of how long my now-meaningless life drags on.

- Jonas Wharton.

The signature was clear this time, as if it had just been written yesterday.

"Well, that explains a lot," Sophie said. "He became a bitter, solitary hermit of a man, consumed by his grief and loneliness. Rotting here all alone."

"Samuel's death must be the 'incident' Ms. Walcott mentioned. The one that made Jonas close the slopes," Maggie said. "And that's why he didn't want this place turned into a ski lodge. And apparently he'll do whatever he feels is necessary, including not resting in peace, to make sure that doesn't happen."

She flipped the scrapbook to its final page.

"It's him!" she cried, pointing at a photo.

The last page of the scrapbook was covered by a large photo of an old man. It was labeled JONAS WHARTON.

"That's the face," Maggie said, jumping up and backing away from the photo as if it might bite her. "*That's* the face of the man I saw in the window the night we arrived!"

"And that's the man who pushed me down the mountain!" Simon added.

"If we had any doubt left, this nails it down," Sophie said, staring at the photo. "We are absolutely dealing with an angry ghost!"

"That's it!" Maggie cried as softly as she could.

"That's what?" Simon asked, truly puzzled.

"We deal with the angry ghost!"

"How do we do that?" Sophie asked, looking back over her shoulder, half expecting the ghost of Old

Man Wharton to pounce at any moment.

"We hold a séance," Maggie explained.

Simon hesitated. "I don't know . . ."

"You have a better idea?" Maggie shot back.

Simon and Sophie looked at Maggie and then shrugged.

"Okay, I'm in," Sophie said.

"Me too," Simon agreed. "I'd like to tell him that pushing people down mountains is definitely not cool!"

"We've got to be fast," Maggie pointed out. "Dinner will be ready soon."

The three kids went to the library and shut the door. This way they'd be close to Jonas's secret room and far enough away from their parents in the kitchen. They sat in a circle on the floor. They placed the scrapbook containing Jonas Wharton's diary in the center of their little circle.

"I read somewhere that if you're trying to contact a spirit, using one of his possessions can help make the connection," Maggie explained.

Then they all grasped hands and closed their eyes.

"Jonas Wharton, we summon you to join us in our circle," Maggie began. "We are truly sorry for your loss and don't wish to cause you any further pain. We know what happened to Samuel. The loss of a brother is a horrible thing to bear. I almost lost my own brother today because you went too far. I'm sure you don't want history to repeat itself, do you?"

Silence filled the room. After a few seconds, Simon spoke.

"Jonas, as the one you could have killed, I ask you to communicate with us," he began. "The reason you tried to stop me from skiing is so that no one can build a ski resort here, so that no one else had to die like Samuel. So why did you try to—"

Simon stopped short and began to make noises that sounded as if he were choking. His eyes closed and his head fell back.

"Simon!" Sophie whispered. "Are you okay?"

She began to pull her hand away from Maggie's, but Maggie held on tight. "Wait!" Maggie said. "Look!"

Simon's head rolled back into an upright position. His eyes opened, revealing only the whites. His mouth trembled; then a voice, not his own, emerged.

"I cannot allow anyone to ski here ever again," said the deep, echoing voice coming from Simon's mouth.

Maggie shook her brother's shoulder. "Simon? Simon?"

"Do not allow skiing here, or more will die!" the deep voice continued.

"Do you mean that they'll die skiing or that you, Jonas Wharton, will kill them?" Sophie asked.

"Do not allow skiing here, or more will die!" Jonas repeated.

"Nobody wants what happened to Samuel to happen—"

"Do not speak that name!" Jonas roared in a voice that filled the room.

"We can't reason with him," Sophie said. "And I'm getting scared that he's hurting Simon again."

"Do you intend to harm my brother?" Maggie asked. "I love him like you loved Samuel."

"DO NOT SPEAK THAT NAME!" Jonas shouted.

Simon's body started twitching wildly.

"We've got to remove Jonas's spirit from Simon's body!" Sophie said. "Let go of my hand—maybe breaking the circle will do it."

Maggie let go of Sophie's hand on one side and Simon's on the other, but Simon kept twitching.

"It's not working!" Sophie cried softly.

Then Maggie got an idea. She grabbed Jonas Wharton's scrapbook, ran down the hallway, across the room, opened the front door, and tossed it out into the snow.

By the time she made it back to the library, Simon had stopped twitching. His head dropped to his chest. Then he raised his head and opened his eyes.

"What just happened?" he asked, clearly himself again, no longer hosting a ghost.

"You were possessed by Jonas Wharton!" Maggie explained, glad that the removal of Wharton's personal item had freed Simon.

"No way!" Simon said, shaking his head and rubbing his eyes. "What'd I, um, he say?"

But there was no time to explain. "Dinner's ready, everyone!" Mrs. Kim shouted from the kitchen.

"It's now or never," Maggie said determinedly. "We have got to convince them, once and for all, not to buy this house!"

# CHAPTER 12

"Who's hungry?" Mr. Kim announced as he strolled into the dining room, carrying a steaming bowl of mac and cheese.

Maggie looked at her father as he scooped some mac and cheese into her bowl. Everything now pointed to the same unbelievable but true conclusion—Old Man Wharton's ghost was doing everything he could to stop the Kims from buying his former home and turning it into a ski resort, because his beloved brother had died here in a skiing accident long ago.

It made perfect sense, but Maggie somehow doubted that her parents would see it that way. After all, it was a pretty far-out story.

"We've got to get some papers from our lawyer back

home this week," Mrs. Kim explained as she gathered a forkful of mac and cheese. "Then we'll come back up here next weekend to finalize the bank loan."

Maggie couldn't stand it any longer. She had to at least try; otherwise by this time next month, she'd be living here with a ghost who'd just tried to kill her brother. Who knew what horrors they'd endure then?

She hoped that this time Simon and Sophie would back her up.

"We can't buy this house!" she announced. "And it's not because I'm a selfish brat who doesn't want to leave her friends."

She glanced at Simon and Sophie. The expressions on their faces told Maggie that they were both wondering how she could present her case without revealing that Simon had disobeyed their parents and gone skiing.

"There is something really wrong with this house," Maggie continued. "You have to believe me."

"I know," her mother said impatiently. "No wi-fi, no cell service, no—"

"No!" Maggie shouted a bit louder than she would have liked. "I know it sounds crazy, but the ghost of Old Man Wharton is haunting this house, because he's determined not to let it become a ski resort."

"Okay, let's say I believed you about the ghost," Mrs. Kim began, "which I'm not saying I do, but for argument's sake, since you seem ready to argue, let's just say that Old Man Wharton's ghost is here. How do you know what he wants or doesn't want? Have you had a conversation with him?"

"Well, yes. We did." Maggie sighed. "We talked with his ghost!"

"Really? And were Simon and Sophie there when you had your little chat?"

All eyes turned to the other two kids. Simon looked at the two girls, then at his mom.

"We all believe Maggie now," Sophie finally said.

"Simon?" Mr. Kim turned to his son.

"I'm with them," Simon replied weakly. "This house is definitely haunted."

"And what do you base this on?" Mrs. Kim asked.

Simon glanced at Maggie and Sophie. He took a deep breath and then began his confession. "I have to tell you guys something, but you're not going to like it," he said to his parents. "I disobeyed you and went skiing today."

"I am so disappointed in you, Simon. I specifically—"

"Wait, Mom, there's more."

Simon proceeded to tell his parents the story of the entire day—how he'd disobeyed his parents, his almost deadly encounter with Old Man Wharton's ghost, and his being possessed at their séance just now.

"There are many reasons you could have fallen, Simon, even though you are a good skier," Mr. Kim spoke up. "Weather conditions, slope conditions . . . but a ghost pushing you? Please. By the way, you're grounded, forever, for disobeying us so blatantly. We really thought we could trust you."

"This nonsense is over," Mrs. Kim said firmly. "We are buying this house. Period. End of conversation."

The rest of dinner passed in uncomfortable silence. When she finished eating, Maggie brought her plate into the kitchen, then headed upstairs. Sophie followed.

"What are we going to do?" Maggie wondered, flopping onto her bed.

"Sorry, Mags. I thought I'd be coming to visit you a lot, but I'm really afraid of this house, and of him."

There was nothing else to say. Maggie felt doomed and terrified about what the future would bring. She rolled over and stared up at the canopy. She felt like crying, but the tears didn't come. Finally she drifted off into an uneasy sleep.

---

"HELP! HELP!"

Maggie was awakened by shouts of terror.

"STOP! HELP ME! SOMEONE HELP ME!"

She sprang from her bed and saw Sophie hurrying toward the bedroom door. She looked out the window. Still dark. Not yet morning.

"What's going on?" Sophie asked.

"HELP!"

"That's Simon!" Maggie cried. "Something's wrong with Simon. Come on!"

The two girls flung the bedroom door open and ran into Mr. and Mrs. Kim in the hallway.

"HELP ME!"

The cries came from downstairs.

"Simon!" Mrs. Kim shouted, dashing down the stairs, followed by the others.

When Maggie reached the bottom of the stairs, she was stunned by what she saw.

Simon was being pulled around the house by an

unseen force. He was awake, his eyes wide with terror. His arms were being jerked back at the elbows, then thrust forward, then pulled back again, as if he were using ski poles to speed himself down a slope.

His knees were locked so that he was moving through the house with his feet scraping along the floor. He was unable to lift his feet or take a step or do anything to slow himself down.

"What's happening?" Maggie shrieked. "Simon!"

"Help me!" Simon cried. "Something's pulling me and dragging me. Forcing me to act like I'm skiing. I can feel it. Stop it. Someone stop it."

Mr. Kim rushed to Simon's side. He reached out to put his arms around his son in an attempt to stop whatever was dragging him around. But before he could reach his son, Mr. Kim was thrown backward, flung away from Simon.

He was knocked off his feet and crashed to the ground ten feet away.

"Paul! Are you all right?" Mrs. Kim cried, rushing to her husband's side.

"It's Old Man Wharton's ghost!" Maggie cried. "He's possessed Simon again!"

She recalled how hiding the scrapbook had broken the spell earlier. She rushed to the front door and pulled it open. The book that had been resting on the snow on the front step was gone!

*Old Man Wharton must have taken it back,* she thought.

Maggie could barely keep herself from screaming and shutting down completely. Her dad had just been tossed across a room like a rag doll. Her brother was still being pulled around the house by something that had taken control of his body. But what? Who? Old Man Wharton? What else could it be?

"LEAVE THIS PLACE . . . NOW!" a voice that wasn't Simon's roared out of his mouth.

"That's him!" Maggie shouted. "That's the voice I've been hearing, telling me to leave. Tell me you all heard it. Tell me!"

"We heard it," Mr. Kim said, climbing to his feet. "I don't know what it is, but—"

"LEAVE THIS PLACE . . . NOW!" the voice repeated out of Simon's mouth, louder this time.

Simon crashed into a wall and collapsed. He popped up immediately and continued his skiing movements.

"Okay, you win!" Mr. Kim cried. "We'll leave. We'll

leave this place and never come back!"

As soon as Mr. Kim uttered the words, Simon was released. He fell to the floor panting and sweating, scared, exhausted, but generally unharmed. His mom helped him up and held him tightly.

"Get your stuff," Mr. Kim ordered everyone. "Pack up, quickly, and let's get out of here. We're leaving. We're done."

Still in shock, Maggie stumbled up the stairs and ran to the bedroom. Sophie was right on her heels. Maggie opened her suitcase and piled her clothes in, then slammed it shut. "That's it for me," she said. "I'll sort this mess out back home, in the suburbs, where we belong."

Sophie shoved her belongings into her backpack and followed Maggie down the stairs.

"Ready?" Mr. Kim asked. He stood at the front door, holding two suitcases. Maggie grabbed her backpack, which had been sitting on the living room floor. She joined the rest of her family outside.

Moments later, Maggie tossed her suitcase into the trunk as her dad started the car. When everyone was inside, he slowly started down the snow-covered driveway.

The morning sun peeked out from behind the big mountain as if to bid the Kims farewell.

"You know, now that I think about it, that house needed too much work anyway," Mrs. Kim said. "And the ski slopes looked too dangerous. The insurance policy alone would cost more than the house. I'm calling the realtor right now and telling her that we're not interested in the house."

She pulled out her cell phone. There was miraculously some service. She dialed the number. "Hello, Ms. McGee, this is Jeannie Kim. We're leaving the Wharton Mansion this minute, and I wanted to tell you that this is most definitely not the property for us. I'll be in touch. Thanks."

In the backseat, Maggie smiled. *I feel like I just won the lottery. Whether they believe in Old Man Wharton's ghost or not really doesn't matter, as long as they don't buy the place.*

As the car reached the end of the long driveway, another car turned in. Maggie spotted ski equipment on the car's roof. A young couple sat in the front seat, with two little boys in the back.

Both cars paused, and the drivers rolled down their windows.

"Hi, are you members of the Wharton family?" the driver asked.

"No, we came to see the old place," Mr. Kim replied. "Just curious."

"Oh, well, Nancy McGee sent us," the woman explained. "My husband and I are looking for a place to turn into a ski resort. This looks wonderful. It's such a pretty location."

"We weren't supposed to arrive until noon, but we're just so excited," the husband added.

Mr. Kim debated with himself about whether to warn this family about the house. What would he say? Would he tell them not to buy the place because it was haunted by a ghost? They'd think he was crazy. Just like he had thought his daughter was crazy.

"Good luck," he simply said, and then he rolled up his window.

As the two cars passed each other, Maggie locked eyes with one of the little boys. She shook her head, hoping to send a message. The boy turned away and started fighting with his brother.

As Mr. Kim started to turn out of the driveway, Maggie turned back for one last look at the mansion.

There, in the same window where she had seen him on the night they arrived, was the ghost of Old Man Wharton. He caught Maggie's eye and smiled, raising his hand to wave good-bye. She wondered if he was sorry for putting her family through such an ordeal this weekend. She wondered if he felt that he did what he had to do in order to keep others safe.

And then he noticed the other car moving up the driveway, approaching the house. His smile morphed into an angry scowl, and he turned from the window to prepare for his new guests.

# DO NOT FEAR—
## WE HAVE ANOTHER CREEPY TALE FOR YOU!

# TURN THE PAGE FOR A SNEAK PEEK AT

You're invited to a

# CREEPOVER®

Don't Drink the Punch!

# PROLOGUE

Mr. Talbert yawned as he tried to hold a stack of uncorrected lab papers and his coffee cup in one hand and unlock his classroom door with the other. Feeble early-morning light filtered through the high windows and reflected off the surfaces of the lab tables. He flicked on the overhead, flooding the room with harsh fluorescent light. He yawned again as he headed for his desk, wondering if he'd have time this Friday morning to finish grading all the labs before first period.

He plopped the stack of papers down on his desk. Then he scratched his head quizzically and regarded the life-size skeleton next to his desk. The skeleton's head was cocked at a jaunty angle. It stared back at him with its shadowy, unseeing eyes.

"Did I just see what I think I saw?" he asked the skeleton.

The skeleton didn't answer.

Mr. Talbert took three backward steps. He turned toward the bug terrarium that sat on the counter running the length of his classroom. The counter was cluttered with mineral samples, animal skulls, and fossils.

The lid of the terrarium was askew. He crouched down to peer into it.

The day before it had contained a bustling little ecosystem, filled with at least a dozen large green scarab beetles, scientific name *Chelorrhina polyphemus*, crawling around on the sandy bottom and gnawing on the bits of apple his middle school students had dropped in. But now the terrarium was empty. The beetles were nowhere to be seen.

Mr. Talbert turned back to the skeleton. "They can't have climbed out on their own," he said. "Someone's taken them!"

The skeleton didn't answer.

# CHAPTER 1

"Um, Jess? No offense, but that hat?" Alice mock-shuddered. "So last year."

Jess reached up and touched her hat, smiling ruefully at Alice. "I know, I know. But it was so cold this morning when I ran out of the house, and I left my good one in my locker at school."

"I always buy two of everything," pronounced Pria. "That way I have a spare."

Kayla, who was picking her way along the icy sidewalk a step behind the other three girls, furrowed her brow. She *liked* Jess's hat. It was a dusty rose color with a folded-up brim that set off Jess's delicate features and wide-set green eyes. But Kayla would never dream of piping up and disagreeing with Alice. No one wanted to invite Alice's criticism if they could help it. Kayla wondered if Pria was serious about buying two of everything. Like *that* would ever happen in Kayla's house. She glanced down at her winter boots, which were very definitely so *two* years ago. Her mom had found them last year at an end-of-season clearance sale, and Kayla had been delighted with them.

"Brrrr!" said Jess, hunkering deeper into her luxurious down coat. "It must be negative a hundred degrees today. Probably a record low for Fairbridge, Minnesota."

"Even Buttercup looks like he feels cold, which is a miracle considering all the natural insulation that dog has," said Alice, gesturing to the dog at the end of the rhinestone-studded leash she was holding in her gloved hand. "My mom says she's going to put him on a diet."

"It's the wind," said Kayla. "That's what makes it feel so cold."

As if to emphasize Kayla's point, an icy gust of crystallized snow sprang up and swirled around the girls. All four put their heads down to shield their faces against the needlelike blast. Kayla could feel the icy snow blowing down the back of her coat collar and up her coat sleeves, which were getting a little too short for her.

"Buttercup! Slow *down*, you dumb dog!" said Alice, lunging forward from the force of the dog's tugging. Buttercup kept straining at his leash.

Kayla usually liked dogs, but Buttercup had to be the ugliest dog she'd ever seen, and he was not especially friendly, either. His snout was all pushed in, as though he had run face-first into a glass patio door. His tail curled up and around backward, so that it practically formed a circle. He didn't walk so much as he waddled, his round belly shifting from side to side. Alice had told her that he was a very rare and valuable breed. Whatever.

Pria adjusted her fuzzy pink earmuffs. "Please tell me why we're out here again?"

"I'm behaving like the model citizen," said Alice with a half smile. "I've offered to walk Buttercup every single afternoon so my parents will stick to their promise to let me have the party."

"It's so awesome that you're going to have a coed Valentine's party," said Pria.

"Yeah, I'm psyched. The girls get to sleep over, and the boys will all leave at eleven," said Alice.

"Will you guys help me find a cute party outfit at the mall today?" asked Jess.

"I'm going to buy at least three outfits," said Alice, ignoring Jess's question. "Then I'll be able to choose whatever I'm in the mood for the day of the party."

"Speaking of shopping," said Pria, "have you *noticed* the stores on this block? I mean, who shops here? Especially considering there's a perfectly good mall nearby."

"Clearly no one, from the looks of these places," said Alice with a sniff.

Kayla clutched the collar of her coat and looked up, squinting as another blast of icy wind sprang up.

It was true. For a generally swanky town like Fairbridge, this seemed to be the one-block-long low-rent district. It was doubly strange that such a run-down block existed in this part of town, of all places, because Alice lived just four blocks away, on one of the fanciest streets in Fairbridge.

They passed an antique store, with a dimly lit storefront displaying a jumble of threadbare old armchairs that looked like they'd seen much better days. Next door was a discount clothing store called Dressed Best, displaying mannequins with no heads or hands, modeling unfashionable dresses. And just past that was a shop with a sign reading ESOTERICA: SPIRITUAL SUPPLIES · CANDLES · OILS · SPELLS. The snow on the sidewalk seemed undisturbed in front of the shops, as though no one had gone in or out in some time.

"Buttercup! I told you to stop *pulling*, you awful little thing," said Alice. "After thousands of dollars of obedience training, he's still the most annoying dog!" She lurched as Buttercup bounded forward, barking his head off at something the girls couldn't see, something behind the recessed door of the dress shop.

"It's a cat," said Pria.

Just then Buttercup managed to slip out of his collar, leaving Alice holding the empty leash. He moved much more quickly on his short legs than Kayla would have thought he could, dashing toward the doorway and yapping furiously.

A black cat streaked across the sidewalk, heading toward the road. Kayla watched, stricken, as it leaped over the mound of plowed, grayish snow and into the road, just as an oncoming car was passing. The cat landed right in front of the car, and the girls couldn't see whether one of the car's tires rolled over it. The driver, a man talking on his cell phone, kept going, apparently unaware of what had happened.

Buttercup struggled to mount the ploughed snow-bank, still in pursuit of the cat, and Alice was able to grab him and snap his collar back on. Then she peered over the edge of the snowbank at the place where the cat had fallen.

"Is it dead?" Jess called to Alice in a small voice.

"Maybe," Alice replied grimly.

The other three girls moved closer to look, peering fearfully over the snowbank.

The cat lay unmoving in a pile of slush.

"Let's get out of here," said Alice. "I so don't need to deal with this right now."

"But what about the cat?" asked Kayla, staring down at it in horror.

"It was probably just a stray," said Jess. "I agree. Let's go."

"It's wearing a collar," Kayla pointed out.

"Come *on*," said Alice. "My mom said she'd take us to the mall as soon as we got back, and it's *freezing* out here."

The other two girls turned to follow Alice. Kayla stood there. "I'm going to check on the cat," she said.

"I'll catch up to you in a minute."

Alice scowled. "Whatever. But hurry up. I can't guarantee that my mom will wait very long."

Kayla watched the other three girls hurry away through the swirling, misting snow. After making sure no cars were coming, she stepped gingerly over the snowbank and looked down at the cat. Its body lay stretched out, its head facing her, its limbs sprawled in an awkward, uncatlike way.

She was afraid to touch it. Was it breathing, or was that just the wind stirring its fur? She crouched down. "Sorry, kitty," she whispered. "I'm sorry about that dumb dog."

She saw no blood, thank goodness, but then, it would be awfully hard to see blood on a coal-black cat like this one. She grew more certain that it was dead. She looked up at the row of stores. Was anyone looking out the window? Even if they had been, they wouldn't be able to see the cat's body, which would be hidden by the bank of snow. She saw no one. She stared back down at the cat.

"I wonder what your name was," she said sadly. And then, as if to answer her, its eyes flew open.

## A Ghostly Message

Jonas Wharton has an important message for you.
Circle every third letter in the long string of letters
on the next page. Then put the circled letters in
order on the line below. The correct letter for the
message is either alphabetically one before or one
after the circled letter. But *A*s will always be *B*s
and *Z*s will always be *Y*s. Can you figure out what
Jonas's message is?

BDTKTSHSBPXZHTBMZ
VBOBQVXCJELSSTTNU
ILISNEJZNSNUAB
CEOPRRDFHLTPCMO

## CIRCLED LETTERS:

_____

_____

## JONAS'S MESSAGE:

_____

_____

# YOU'RE INVITED TO ...
## CREATE YOUR OWN SCARY STORY!

Do you want to turn your sleepover into a creepover? Telling a spooky story is a great way to set the mood. P. J. Night has written a few sentences to get you started. Fill in the rest of the story and have fun scaring your friends.

You can also collaborate with your friends on this story by taking turns. Have everyone at your sleepover sit in a circle. Pick one person to start. She will add a sentence or two to the story, cover what she wrote with a piece of paper, leaving only the last word or phrase visible, and then pass the story to the next girl. Once everyone has taken a turn, read the scary story you created together aloud!

Once upon a time there was a young girl who lived all alone in a small cabin on a cold, snowy mountain. Her only company was the coyotes and the howling of the wind. She longed to leave this place and meet other girls her age, but she was trapped in the cabin by a mean old . . .

_____

_____

_____

_____

_____

_____

_____

_____

_____

_____

_____

_____

_____

_____

THE END

A lifelong night owl, **P. J. NIGHT** often works furiously into the wee hours of the morning, writing down spooky tales and dreaming up new stories of the supernatural and otherworldly. Although P. J.'s whereabouts are unknown at this time, we suspect the author lives in a drafty, old mansion where the floorboards creak when no one is there and the flickering candlelight creates shadows that creep along the walls. We truly wish we could tell you more, but we've been sworn to keep P. J.'s identity a secret . . . and it's a secret we will take to our graves!

# What's better than reading a really spooky story?

## Writing your own!

You just read a great book. It gave you ideas, didn't it? Ideas for your next story: characters…plot…setting… You can't wait to grab a notebook and a pen and start writing it all down.

It happens a lot. *Ideas just pop into your head.* In between classes entire story lines take shape in your imagination. And when you start writing, the words flow, and you end up with notebooks crammed with your creativity.

*It's okay, you aren't alone.* Come to **KidPub**, the web's largest gathering of kids just like you. Share your stories with thousands of people from all over the world. Meet new friends and see what they're writing. Test your skills in one of our writing contests. See what other kids think about your stories.

And above all, *come to write!*

**www.KidPub.com**